The Grave Keeper

ALL HALLOWS

EBONY OLSON

EBANDMUSE & PUBLICATIONS

EBANDMUSE
PUBLICATIONS

Published 2022

Published by EbandMuse Publications, Sydney, Australia

Copyright © 2022 by **Ebony Olson.**

Paperback: 9780645157925

Cover by Strange Angel Designs

Edited by Striding Ibis

http://ebonyolson.com/

The Ghost Tour

〜

COLD TASMAN SEA WATERS CARESSED MY FEET. Closing my eyes, I let the nearness of the ocean calm me. My morning visit to an old convict settlement had turned out to be more disturbing than I could predict. Not only was the horror of the way the convicts were treated blanketing the buildings, but the lingering fear and misery of a more recent time saturated the air. It wasn't until the tour guide explained the meeting point was the site of a mass shooting that I understood my need to hide behind a tree. Tonight, I would return to that hell hole for a ghost tour. Maybe I'd have better luck finding what I was looking for then.

"Hey!" A surfer who had braved the cold came out of the water with his board under his arm. "The tide's coming in. If you stay any longer, you'll be waist-deep in water trying to get back through the cave. Come on."

He walked on, muttering about tourists under his breath.

Getting to my feet, I gave the ocean one more longing look, then headed for the opening in the cliff face, which formed the Remarkable Cave. The colors inside were what made the caves so different. The rock walls were burgundy at the base, then variegated with pink, lavender, yellow, green, and even blue near the ceiling. As I trudged back through the knee-deep water streaming through the cave, I admired the natural rainbow rock.

As I got halfway into the cave, the current wrapped around my legs and tugged hard as it pulled out to sea. Yep, the surfer was right. Had I waited much longer, I would have struggled to get back. Looking over his shoulder when he reached the viewing platform, the guy stopped and offered me his hand to help me up.

"You all right?" he asked.

"Yes, thank you."

Giving me a nod, he let me go ahead of him up the hundred and thirty stairs back to the road—I'd counted them on the way down. Stopping at the bench, I put my sneakers on while I watched the surfer strip out of his wetsuit, and wrap a towel around his waist before removing the lower half. He had a great smile, shaggy hair, and a lovely physique. He wasn't standout good-looking, but that smile could make up for the slightly crooked nose and broad forehead.

"Where's your car?" he asked as he pulled on a pair of shorts under his towel.

"Oh, I walked here."

Lifting an eyebrow, his eyes scanned me from head to toe. "Did you want a lift back to where you are staying?"

Sadly for this guy, I was still hung up on my ex. Which is what brought me here in the first place, because I'd been told that places that were hell on Earth were portals to the realm of Hell.

"Sorry, what's your name?"

Wetting his lips, the surfer beamed his smile my way. "David."

Sure it was. "Thank you, David, but I need the alone time, and I find long walks are good for my soul."

"You're sure?"

"Yes, thank you. It was kind of you to offer." That scored me a smirk and a shake of his head.

Then, to prevent making it evident that I was waiting for him to leave, I took my time getting my headphones connected to my phone.

With a slight frown, the surfer finally got in his car and left. He was probably wondering why his charm didn't work on me.

An hour after sunset, I let myself in through the cute pedestrian gate at the back entrance to the convict settlement. While there were still many tourists around today, I was the only one from the bed and breakfast who wanted to do the ghost tour.

Walking up the roadway in front of the cute cottages that once housed essential settlement members, I wondered where I was meant to meet the tour group. Unfortunately, the ticket didn't come with instructions.

Two men stood talking up ahead. Before I got close, I made sure their clothing was modern. I'd already gotten a few weird looks during the day tour when I excused myself to get by a lady, only to realize that her dress was a few centuries out of date.

One of the men wore a suit—a bit over the top for a ghost tour, but maybe he was management—and the other wore chinos with a heavy metal t-shirt.

"Excuse me," I interrupted politely, earning me raised brows from them both.

Damn, they were hot. Like, the kind of hot you usually

only see in magazines or in movies. They had similar features and the same intense dark blue gaze, which stripped you of your flesh and bones until your soul stood naked and randy before them. The dark-haired one was almost the spitting image of my first lover. But it wasn't him.

Clearing my throat, I wondered if maybe they were paid actors for the tour. Like we'd get to see them in rags and locked in the stocks getting whipped later. Okay, that was probably wishful thinking.

"Do you know where the ghost tour gathers to start?"

Slowly, their faces relaxed, and they looked at each other before the very handsome blond in the suit cocked a bold brow above his blue eyes and indicated the garden just down the retaining wall. "In the rose garden. You can find the stairs opposite the last cottage."

"Thank you." Stepping by them, I tried not to notice how they both turned and watched me walk on before whispering to each other.

Instead of being creeped out, I felt my cheeks heat. I even tucked my hair behind my ear, all flirty-like, when I sneaked another look as I headed down the stairs, only to find them following me.

Damn, was this part of the country full of murderers? Seriously, that was my type. Well, men likely to become evil incarnate and alphaholes were definitely my thing. My most recent ex turned out to be a serial killer. Not that I knew until after the car accident that killed us. I had knocked down a box of his while quickly packing a few things.

An assassin, I could cope with, had managed with previously. But a serial killer for whom I fit the victim profile—young, dark-haired, and educated. To know for some reason he could rise above his mental health issues and resist his impulses with me, but kill others who looked like me, that still messed with me.

My ex had never hurt me. On the contrary, he'd absolutely adored me. Still, every family deserves closure. I sent the box with the map marking where he'd disposed of the bodies and the photos and trophies he'd taken to the police anonymously. Then I'd put my things in storage again, assumed a new identity, and started my tour of hell holes.

While we waited for the tour to start, I gazed over the grounds. Why I expected an ominous red glow to be emanating from the doorway of some building, I don't know. Still, I was hoping the door to Hell would come with a beacon, some neon signage, and possibly a doorbell.

"Okay, I think everyone is here. Can you all gather around?" A man in the tour uniform called. "My name is Jamie. I'm your tour guide. Who wants to see a ghost tonight?"

Nearly every person put their hand up, keen for the excitement of seeing through the veils. Only the two men I'd asked for directions and I kept our hands down. Speaking of the panty-drenching brothers—they had to be related—they looked at me calculatingly. The blond gave me a small smile and a knowing nod.

"I don't," Jamie continued a little softer, letting his voice turn eerie. The hands started falling as confusion settled over their faces. "I've been told by those who do that once you see one, you see all; here, the majority are not nice."

Well, that was true. The blond's eyes returned to me and gave me a wink. Not creepy at all.

As we made our way to the ruined church, the village was calm and peaceful; it was the exact opposite of the daytime. The day visit had suffused me with anguish and vulnerability. So, I focused on the peacefulness of what was a visually beautiful place.

The bell tower yielded the first flinch, giving me the sudden need to put my back to the wall and avoid stepping inside the structure. The thing about the lingering dead is that they notice those subtle shifts, those wary glances. They float closer and breathe down your neck, observe the shiver that vibrates through your body; they see it and know.

"You okay?" The blond whispered as the others moved on. "You look a little hesitant."

Forcing a smile, I waved it away. "Yes, of course."

You'd think I'd be used to it, and in most places, I can ignore the small things that set your hair on end, but the sporadic evil of this location had my adrenaline pumping.

Despite his smile, the blond's eyes told me he didn't believe me. "I'm Lucas. This is my younger brother Aureus. You can hang with us if it makes you feel safer."

What disturbed me was that something was comforting about the brothers. Terrifying and cozy all at once. Especially the tall, dark-haired, and quiet Aureus. Yes, that's how off my taste in men seemed to be. Maybe it was this place that made them seem safe in comparison.

"I'm good." I excused myself and walked faster to catch up with the group.

Lucas snickered, and Aureus elbowed him. Returning to my search for a portal of Hell, I tried to ignore them. It was hard to do. They both had a presence that loomed over you, making you feel them even when they weren't touching you. The similarity of their appearance to the angel I'd once known and the vibe they gave off couldn't be ignored, especially when they were standing next to me at each of the stops.

I saw the first ghost at the priest's house. Another sick fuck in a long history of human monsters, he'd taken in young female convicts as his housekeepers, and then used them as his personal slaves. I almost vomited in my mouth when Jamie went into detail. Over the eons that I'd lived I'd seen humans do horrible things, but when they hurt children, it made my stomach twist in knots.

Circling the room, the Priest noticed the pretty young woman standing beside me and suddenly appeared behind her, whispering all the vile things he'd do in her ear.

Despite not knowing why, the girl trembled at his touch on her bare shoulder, gripping her boyfriend's hand tightly. When Jamie indicated we should make our way out, the girl ran for the exit, causing her boyfriend to hit the wall beside the door in her desperation to get away.

Aureus shook his head at the Priest, who scowled back and vanished. Then Aureus was observing me again and I had to force myself not to react to the fact he could not only see ghosts, but they seemed to know each other.

"You see them," he stated quietly as he fell in beside me.

"See who?" I feigned ignorance.

He chuckled, a sweet and low sound that made the hair on the back of my neck stand up and things tighten down below. Gods, I thought Lucas had an effect on me, but Aureus's voice was better than any non-physical foreplay I'd ever experienced.

Exiting the house, the brothers watched me intently. Pretending to ignore them, I took in the view down to the bay. Aureus stepped right up behind me.

"We see you," he whispered.

Oh, Gods. I was going to come just with the sound of his voice.

"Right, let's move on. The last house on the right, please," Jamie announced in a clear, cheery voice, but he tilted his head as he observed me.

Everyone started walking. Lucas held out his hand for me to take, the pupil of his eyes flashing red. Shaking my head slightly, I stepped sideways to avoid him and jogged down the stairs to catch up with the other tourists. Lucas loosed a deep and low, menacing-to-my-panties chuckle behind me.

A woman fell in beside me, her smooth and noiseless gait a clear giveaway on the gravel path.

"You're pretty. There's a party tomorrow night for spirits who want to connect with humans again." She looked over her shoulder. "Or if Angels are your thing...."

She gave me a saucy wink. Angels. Well, that explained why Aureus was so familiar. Considering the first person I had any memory of was an Angel who looked just like Aureus, maybe Lucas wasn't his only brother.

"Go away, Isabelle. She's not what you think." Aureus ordered sternly from the other side of me, making me jump.

Frowning at me, Isabelle cocked her head to the side to study me, then vanished. *You and me both, Sister.* I'd had eons to try and figure it out and I still had no clue as to what I was.

Aureus clasped my hand in his, holding firmly, so I couldn't pull away without attracting unwanted attention. Not that I could pull away. His hand in mine was two super magnets stuck together, and the way it affected me physiologically was pure euphoria.

"How unusual," Aureus murmured, sounding in awe, as if he too felt it.

By the time we caught up with the others, my panties were drenched, my blood was on fire, and my heart was in my throat. The need in me was something I'd never experienced before, but I knew already this was not the first time Aureus had touched me.

Jamie directed everyone around the back at the last house, stopping above the steps that led to a basement. During the day, I'd walked past these stairs and refused to go down there. There was no way in Hell I was descending those steps at night. Knowing my luck, that's where the door I was seeking was hidden, but I couldn't bring myself to check it out.

"So, what are you?" Isabelle jumped around beside me like she had ants in her pants.

She was really hyperactive for a ghost.

"Isabelle," Aureus growled.

"It's a really great party. Lots of good food, alcohol, and fucking. You like fucking, right?"

My eyebrows lifted at how direct she was.

"Isabelle! Excuse us!" Aureus and Lucas grabbed her and dragged her back to the front yard to scold her.

My eyes bugged as I struggled not to gawk that they could physically grab and pull a ghost. Not that I'd ever tried manhandling one.

Suddenly, my heart was pounding in my chest, white noise buzzing in my ears as I watched the two fuck-worthy angels school the ghost. Doubling my concern, I couldn't tell if I was panicking or horny. This was not good.

Maybe I should give up on finding Hell and go home. It'd been a century. I was overdue to spend time at the temple.

"Is anyone claustrophobic?" Jamie asked.

Without hesitation, I put my hand up. Tilting his head, Jamie gave me a look of interest.

"I'll wait up here," I announced, settling myself on the garden wall.

Glancing around as everyone else headed down the stars, Jamie came closer. "Are you sure you will be alright up here by yourself?"

"What's down there?"

"The morgue. This was the doctor's house. Down there is where he conducted his experiments and not only on the dead."

The excruciating pain and terror seeping from that place made sense now. I was probably passing up my chance of finding the door to Hell, but it was too much for me to endure.

"Actually, I think I'll head off. The tours have been great. I'm just tired and would prefer to get back before it gets too late."

"Are you staying nearby?"

"Just across the road," I pointed to the lane with the little gate I could shortcut back to my lodgings through.

Sighing, Jamie nodded. "Well, get back safely."

Turning, he followed everyone downstairs out of sight. As soon as none of them were visible, I ran.

Getting back to my hotel, I took a moment to gather myself. No one had followed me, the night was calm, I was okay. Just a really unusual encounter. Still, the smart thing would be to move on quickly. Checking in with the owner, I let them know I'd be leaving at dawn and not to bother with my breakfast. After that, I spent a long time in the shower, trying to cleanse myself of the negative energies from the day.

Packing my things, I set my bag by the door, keeping my toiletries and clothes for tomorrow in the bathroom. Then I sat down with my list and worked out where I should go next. I'd always wanted to visit Tasmania, so I decided some sightseeing before continuing my search would be okay. It's not like Hell was going anywhere. After deciding on a trip up the coast, I turned out the light and slept.

A deep chuckle and those flickering red pupils invaded my dream. A warm hand caressed me like a lover, making me moan and ache for something I'd not experienced in decades since I last left the temple of pleasure.

Waking in the darkness, I startled, pulse racing. The strong arm around me tightened in comfort, and I sighed in relief, snuggling into the hard body behind me.

"I dreamed we died," I whispered.

"Not yet," the voice whispered in reassurance.

Grateful, I pressed closer to him, shifting his hand up to grasp my breast like he always liked to hold me. Behind me, he moaned and chuckled.

"Johnny," I sighed.

"Who's Johnny?"

My spine froze at the question, waking me finally. When I

tried to roll away, his arm became a restraint, so the only way I could move was to turn and face him.

Swallowing hard, I turned in his arms, praying in my head it was another nightmare, that someone wasn't here. Because Johnny was dead.

No such luck.

The light through the window revealed David, the surfer. Adrenaline raced through me like a bullet through my heart, affecting my breathing but freezing me in fear. Yes, I'd been murdered countless times before, but that didn't make me cavalier about suffering first. For sure, David was no incubus sneaking into my bed for sex and feeding before leaving me alive with a tender kiss.

Caressing my cheek, he pulled me tight against him, staring into my eyes.

"Don't look so scared. If you are nice to me, when we are done, I'll set you free," his eyes glimmered.

His lips brushed mine, then firmed over my mouth, giving me the most delicate of kisses. Did that bullshit reassure his victims?

"No!"

When I tried shoving him away, he tightened his hold, laughing.

Shifting his weight, he rolled, and I fought his attempt to pin me.

"You've got spirit; I'll give you that," he chuckled while I struggled against him.

After a few minutes, he'd had enough.

A sharp pain pierced my stomach, stopping me in my fight, my eyes staring wide into the evil above me. My breath came in short pants of ragged pain radiating through my abdomen and chest.

"Did you know stomach wounds are one of the slowest ways to die? Excruciatingly painful but terribly slow." Putting his hand over my mouth, he yanked the flick knife free. The agony roared through my insides and out of my mouth. "Plenty of time for me to have fun."

Heat built inside of me, my rage and fear burning through my blood. This sensation, I knew well. I'd been through it many times, though usually it happened with my last breath. Maybe it was because it had only been a few months since my most recent resurrection. Still, there was no way I was going to survive just to have this bastard keep killing me while he played with me.

Summoning my fury to my hand, I yelled all my indignation into his laughing face as I slammed my fist against his chest. Sunlight exploded between us, blinding us both as the sudden radiance lit up the room.

My attacker went limp and rolled from me. Getting off the bed quickly, I put my back to the wall, ready to fend him off again. Darkness suffused back into its space, until the golden light was only a faint glow on the bed and coming from my abdomen. The room was quiet. Nothing moved. Panting in pain, I found the light switch.

On the bed, the surfer was staring up at the ceiling blankly, a golden ray of light impaling his chest. My eyes bugged out of my head, breathing became near impossible. Then, slowly, the light dissolved, the last of it fading away from both of us along with my pain. I still had to be dreaming. I'd never summoned my light into a weapon before.

"Well, that was new."

"What the...?" Spinning around, Lucas sat on the sofa, legs crossed, forehead furrowed as he studied the body on my bed.

"She sent him straight to Hell, too. Not an ounce of his evil soul left for you to collect."

Movement brought my attention to Aureus, who stood right next to me. Before I could blink, he caught me up in his arms and kissed me. His lips were toasty warm marshmallows, and the sense of belonging hit me like a freight train. Some tightness I'd always had inside of me eased. It was like I'd spent an eternity waiting for this moment.

"Better make it quick. Someone might have heard her," Lucas suggested.

Not that I was paying attention. This was hands down the best kiss I'd ever experienced.

Something shifted inside me, tore open, and lurched towards Aureus. Jolting from the sudden heartache, I tried to push him away, to fight, but he had my arms pinned to his chest. There was nothing I could do. The moments of agony and betrayal before I woke up on the steps of a temple thousands of years ago played out in my head as if it was happening again.

Freaking out as the sense of Aureus grew to encompass me, I lifted my eyes to meet his one more time as a lone tear escaped my eye. Then a supernova exploded through the room, and I was lost to it, to him, to everything.

The House Beside the Grave

THE ROOM WAS BEAUTIFULLY DECORATED IN WHITE and gold, the bed large and ornate but not overly gaudy. My bag sat on the ottoman along the foot of the bed. My toiletries and the clothes I'd left out for tomorrow were in the bathroom waiting for me. It was like I went to sleep in a cheap bed and breakfast and woke up in a luxury hotel.

Pulling back the sheer curtains, this room overlooked the ocean. The sun was high overhead, indicating I'd slept through the better part of the day.

"Where am I?"

Another set of windows looked over a lighthouse on a small island, halfway between the heads of what looked to be a harbor inlet. The day was clear and the water calm. I could easily see the navy blues of deep water forming a channel through the heads and how it contrasted with the paler shallows over the reef that stretched from the other side of the island across the harbor.

Wherever I was, it was beautiful. I just didn't know if this was safe. Approaching the door, I caught my reflection in the mirror. My pajamas were ruined with blood and the hole from my attacker's flick knife. It probably wouldn't hurt to freshen up a little first.

Going to the bathroom, I undressed and started the shower. Washing clean, I made sure my abdomen was whole, and all the dried blood scrubbed away.

Dressed and determined to find out what had become of me, I tried the door, fully expecting I'd find it locked. Instead, it turned in my hand. It opened out onto a balcony over-looking a massive void to the jaw-dropping mosaic floor one level below. Gripping the ornate golden railing, I followed it to the curved stairs, all the time keeping my eyes on the staff moving around, who seemed to be setting up for a function.

No one paid me any attention when I reached the ground floor, making me glad I'd chosen to wash and change first. Everyone was busy rushing here and there, except for one lady who stood in the center of the chaos directing deliveries or inquiries.

Before I could open my mouth and ask directions, a familiar figure stepped in front of me. "Isabelle?"

"Morning, Danse." She smiled, looping her arm through mine.

My jaw dropped open. Not only was she freezing cold to touch, but she used that name. It was the first name I'd ever had and hadn't been used in a very long time.

"Aureus is having breakfast. Let's not get in the party plan-ner's way. They have a lot to do before the masked ball tonight."

"Isn't it afternoon?"

"Yes, but you only just woke up, and Aureus tends to sleep all day."

Pushing through a door, we arrived in a grand kitchen, complete with a chef directing his staff where to put the arriving food. Across the far side of the room, Aureus sat at a breakfast nook set in a bay window. When we arrived at the table, he put aside his book and smiled up at me. Cue my knees going weak and my girly bits screaming like hardcore K-Pop fans when their favorite group steps on stage.

"Danse, you're awake." Aureus stood and placed a kiss on my cheek before indicating the chair beside him. "Join me. Are you hungry?"

"I'm more confused."

"I'm sure you have any questions, but let's get you fed first." Then, making a gesture to the chef, Aureus corralled me into the chair. "How did you sleep?"

"Was I sleeping?"

"Eventually," Aureus answered. Noticing Isabelle hovering, he made a shooing gesture. "Don't you have a party to organize?"

Rolling her eyes, Isabelle strode out of the room.

"She's substantial today."

"All Hallows Eve. All the spirits wandering the realm of the living will seem as alive as ever."

"She's still cold."

"She is dead. Warmth is a perspective and need of those with beating hearts."

Was I dead? I put my hand to my chest.

Smirking, Aureus took a sip of his coffee. "You are alive, Danse. Though, I wonder how?"

"I gave up on trying to figure that out a long time ago. Why did you come to my room?"

"To collect the soul you dispatched, of course. The fact that it brought me back to you is a bonus. Unfortunately, we didn't arrive until he had already harmed you, so we had to let things play out. We are forbidden to interfere with humans while they live. I had to let your would-be-killer's fate run its course."

"So, you would have just sat there and watched while he tortured me to death?"

"I've watched humans do the vilest things. But, if it's any consolation, I wouldn't have enjoyed it."

"Not really."

Smirking, Aureus leaned back in his seat and watched me. My body warmed as his gaze swept over me, making me shift in my seat. The chef deposited two plates of breakfast in front of us, put a basket of freshly baked croissants on the table, and then brought us both fresh coffee.

The entire time, I was swamped with visions of Aureus laying me in his lap and rubbing his hands over me. The familiarity of him, of his hands, was something I could never have prepared myself for.

Clearing my throat, I got my mind away from how Aureus affected me and focused on the issue. "Where am I?"

"My home."

"Which is where?"

Gazing out the window at the small lighthouse and reef beyond, Aureus picked up his fresh coffee. "This is the Grave Gate. That is not the name of the town that the humans consider this house to exist in, but the answer for people like you and me, Danse, is as I just named it. The opening to that harbor out there is Hell's Gate. Both in the Epoch realm and the celestial."

"People like you and me?" I questioned. Could this man finally have answers for me?

"Hmm, maybe that was too broad. You are not human, but you are not one of my kind, yet you are celestial in origin. The light that saved you last night was definitely forged by spirit fire. The eternal flame that burns still in Yahweh's old temple. Instead of ash, it creates spirits. You, however, are not the residue of the flame but forged of the flame itself."

Seriously? That's the answer? It doesn't tell me what I am or why I keep living.

"What the hell does that mean?"

Inhaling, Aureus set his cup aside.

"I don't know. The only items I've seen forged of spirit fire before have been our weapons. So, the best answer I can derive is that you are not human, nor angel, but you are heavenly." Gazing at my lips, his mouth twitched. "Especially when I have my hands and lips on you."

A gentle heat raced through me at the memory and his flirting. Heavenly wasn't the term I'd associate with the kind of desire this man evoked in me. More deliciously sinful and dirty lust, full of need and the intention to do horribly good things to each other.

"Why did you bring me here? What are your intentions?"

"Ah." Aureus eyed me. "Yes, I suppose that is important." Then, picking up the tongs, he placed a croissant on both our plates. "If I answer it, will you eat?"

The food did smell delicious. Picking up the knife, I opened the croissant and started slathering it with the fresh lemon butter on the table.

Satisfied, Aureus started prepping his pastry. "You saw us. Even humans with divining abilities who can see through the veils can't see us unless we want them to. They may perceive us, but not as one of them, and none would ever ask us directions.

"As soon as you did, we looked into your soul for an answer. But the thing is, you don't have one."

"I don't?" *Well, hell! That's not something I expected to hear.*

"You don't. Again, only those who are the by-product of the spirit fire are born with souls, which discounted you as an Epoch entity. You're not one of us, so we were fascinated by you. But you disappeared on us. Lucas was hunting you while I went to collect the evil soul that would die that night, and we both ended up in your room. The situation we witnessed only further increased our curiosity. You are forged of spirit fire, but you are not a weapon. So, what are you?"

"Immortal."

"All of us without souls are. That is the physics of it. But tell me more."

"Tell me why you brought me here."

"Did you want us to leave you with the dead body to be discovered at dawn?"

Mouth falling open, I slouched back in my seat. "They are going to think I killed him."

"You did."

"But it was self-defense. They won't think that. The police will be looking for me."

"Actually, the way you killed him looks like a heart attack. Still, there was your blood everywhere. You have changed your identity how many times now? I presume it won't be an issue to do it again if you choose to return to the Epoch realm."

Huffing, I picked up the coffee and took a sip. "I do miss the days where you just moved towns and gave them a new name. Now there are fingerprints, retinal scans, and all those security measures to account for when creating a new identity."

"How long have you lived?"

Inhaling, I considered the view out the window. "I'm not sure. I feel like I've been here since the beginning of time, but that's probably not the case. Long enough that I stopped counting my resurrections centuries before Jesus made a name for himself. In my time, I have watched empires rise and fall, and the world remake itself several times over."

Pensive, I ate my breakfast. Aureus observed me, peppering me with questions about my past and abilities. He seemed disappointed that last night was the first time I'd used the light inside me as a weapon. Finally, he seemed like he'd run out of questions, but I still had one for him.

"You didn't tell me your intentions for me." I reminded him as he stood to leave.

Smirking, Aureus leaned over me, his fingers brushing along my jaw, making me sigh a little from that unique connection of his skin on mine. "I want you to be my date for the party tonight."

"Party?"

"Yes. Isabelle invited you, remember?"

"Are there any rituals or sacrifices performed at this party? Because I've been there and done that, and I have to say, I wasn't a fan."

Lifting a brow, Aureus met my eyes. His pupils were a moonless night at sea, with a distant flash from the lighthouse onshore. "It is my annual Halloween masked ball to celebrate the thinning of the veils, where the dead and the living may join together in celebration."

"That's all?"

Rubbing his thumb across my lips, Aureus lowered his mouth to my ear. "It's a start." He dropped the barest of kisses to my pulse. "Who knows where it will end."

My breath rushed out in a torrent of sexual need and desire, but Aureus pulled away and took up my hand. "Let's go find you a dress."

❖

All Hallows Eve

THE EVENT MANAGER HAD A RACK OF BALL GOWNS and evening dresses waiting for us. Taking a seat in a cozy reading chair, Aureus insisted I try every dress before making a choice. Finally, after I tried everything on, Aureus stood up, moved to the 'keep' rack, and pulled out the rose-gold ball gown.

"This one." It was my favorite too. "The party starts in two hours. I've asked a stylist to assist you. I'll let them know you are ready for them."

As Aureus turned to walk away, I couldn't wonder anymore. "Have we met before? I could have sworn...you're so familiar to me."

Stopping, Aureus turned his chin to his shoulder but didn't look at me. "No. At least, not in a way that I would recognize you, but I feel the sentiment, Danse. When I touch you, it's like I've held you all my life."

"I know every hand that's ever wielded me. Can recognize them as if their fingerprints are absorbed into my system. You had me once; I know it at my core. It's ancient and yet still so fresh. Are you the one who left me at the temple?"

Frowning, Aureus turned to me then. "Temple?"

"My first memory is waking on the steps of a temple. I was naked, bruised, and aching terribly. There was a man there. He looked like you, but he had the same reddish pupils that Lucas has. He took me and gave me to an ancient god. That is where I started my life—as a god's concubine. Dion was the one to give me the name of Danse. The first name I existed as."

Furrowing his forehead, Aureus came closer. "The temple, did it have a fire at the top?"

Closing my eyes, I remembered those first moments. It was patchy after all this time, out of focus in parts. "Yes. It was a strange fire. A clear flame almost."

With his pupils almost pinpoint, Aureus stepped closer again. "It couldn't be...."

Caressing my arms from wrist to shoulder, I closed my eyes as my body hummed to the wonder of his touch. Slipping a hand to the back of my neck, Aureus rubbed his hand along my spine, making me smile.

Opening my eyes, I stared into his happily. "My body knows your touch. You owned me, didn't you?"

Mouth hanging open as he gazed at me in wonder, Aureus stared into my eyes. "I didn't abandon you. They took you from me to punish me. If you are what I think you are, then I have longed for you since the fall of angels."

Using his hand on my spine, Aureus pressed me firmly to him, his other hand mapping the contours of my face, testing the plumpness of my lips.

"After all this time, could it be?" he murmured, then his lips closed over mine.

The kiss was everything I remembered from the night before. My body buzzed with recognition and wanton desires. When I pressed the kiss further, Aureus pulled away gently.

We stood there staring into each other's eyes a moment

longer before he extricated himself from me. "I must speak to Lucas. He will derive the truth of this."

"How?"

"If you are what I believe, you'll react to him just as much as me."

"Why?"

"Because he forged you for me to wield." Taking one more longing look, Aureus turned for the bedroom door. "Get ready for the party and wait here for me to collect you."

The clicking of the door after he left the room left me just as confused as when I woke up here, but I hoped Lucas may have the answers we needed.

The knock at the door broke me free of my daydreams. Turning from the window that overlooked the treacherous reef, I went to the door and opened it. Leaning on the rail of the balcony, Aureus looked dashing in pure black. The cloak he wore covered him nearly entirely, wrapping shoulder to shoulder and sweeping down to the top of his black boots. His face was half-hidden behind a black bone mask that covered from his forehead to just below his nose. His dark blue eyes seemed magnetizing, surrounded by all his darkness.

"You look beautiful," Aureus complimented me as he took in my appearance.

Heat rushed through my blood as Aureus came forward to stand before me.

Tilting his head, a bare arm escaped through a slit in the side of the cloak to caress the delicate filigree rose gold mask that surrounded my eyes. "The rose brings out the gold in your eyes. Last night they seemed quite pale when the light caught them, but tonight I see they reflect the light, and only when someone is standing right before you can your worth be seen."

"People always tell me my eyes are weird."

"Mortals don't know better." Offering me his arm, he half turned. "Shall we?"

"Are you naked beneath that cloak?"

Side of his mouth lifting, Aureus straightened and threw open his cloak, so it hung off both of his shoulders. His defined physique was breathtaking. Only his lower half was covered by some expensive-looking suit pants.

"Wow," I breathed.

I'd seen gorgeous men before, gods even, but there was something about Aureus that made my body hum with longing. Then, realizing I was actually humming vocally, I shut it off and cleared my throat, trying not to appear impressed and clearly failing.

Stepping closer, Aureus backed me up against the frame of the door. Leaning into me, he smiled. Slipping his hand around my waist, Aureus traced my exposed spine from the base to my neck. The dress was backless, held on at the shoulders by a chain of appliqué that buttoned behind my nape.

"Are you wearing underwear?"

Wetting my lips, I swallowed hard. "Yes."

"Take it off."

"Uh-"

"Off, Danse. Now."

Biting my lip, I scrunched up the satin skirt of the dress. As it got to mid-thigh, Aureus eased back and looked down. Dropping his hands, he slid up the exposed skin of my thighs and gripped the sides of the skin-toned seamless scanties, and yanked them down, letting them fall around my ankles.

Careful to free my strappy heels of the material, I stepped out and went to pick them up. Getting in my way, Aureus took my wrist in his hand and started walking for the stairs.

"Leave them there." Hooking my hand into his elbow, he drew his cloak closed, and down the stairs to the party we went.

Hours later, I sat on a lounge beside Aureus set to one side of the house's great room. This room itself was the size of my last place and reminded me of my days at court centuries ago. The room was full of people in all sorts of Halloween regalia. All of them were masked, either physically or painted on. The only way I could tell human from spirit was the coldness in the eyes of the dearly departed.

"Are they earth-bound ghosts?" I asked Isabelle, who lounged on the ottoman next to our love seat.

"Some. The veil is so thin that there is no difference between the land of the living and the dead tonight. So, some are also what you might call 'crossed over'."

"Are any from Hell?"

"You need to think of the celestial realm like its epoch twin. Those who live in the summer fields or whatever name you give the afterlife are free to wander wherever. Just as a human can travel from town to town. Hell is the equivalent of a labor camp or prison. Spirits who are judged to deserve it are sent there to pay their penance. Once they serve their time, they can wander the summer fields as well as the rest of them."

"Them? You are not one of them?"

Glaring past me to Aureus, Isabelle huffed. "I never crossed. I never will."

"Why?" I asked as she rose from her seat.

"Because if you cross, you eventually reincarnate. Living was the equivalent of hell for me. I never want to go through it again. Aureus can't promise I wouldn't, so I refused to go. Plus, I'd have to spend a good century or more in hell first, being tortured for my sins. Hard pass." Looking across the room, her face morphed into annoyance. "Great, the Prince of Hell is here. Way to make everyone uncomfortable, Aurie."

"You know, Isabelle. You get two days a year to have fun and interact with the living, and you're wasting it bitching about my guest list. Go find a pretty human and have a good time."

With another huff, Isabelle swanned into the guests, walking straight for a stunning blonde. Whispering something in her ear, Isabelle smiled, then led the woman onto the dance floor to sway along with the others currently bumping and grinding to the heavy dance beat.

"Evening," Lucas greeted us as he cleared the crowd.

He wore an Armani suit, much like the night we met, except he was shirtless tonight and wore a goat's skull, horns and all, as a hat. He was painted to look like his upper face and chest had been splattered with deep red blood, the droplets even glistening in the light. Okay, I hoped it was paint.

"Well, don't you look like a shining beacon of celestial temptation." Lucas surveyed me before taking a seat on the other side of Aureus.

"You made it?" Aureus waved over a waiter carrying a tray of alcoholic cocktails as colorful as the guests' costumes and potent as all hell—forgive the term. I'd had two on arrival and giggled for a good hour afterward at absolutely everything and nothing. I hadn't been that off my face since my days in France mixing opium and absinthe.

"I did. I went to the temple and paid the flame a visit."

"What was the answer?"

"Nothing forged of celestial light and eternal flame can ever be destroyed, only reforged."

"So, I'm right?"

"We can find out." Eyeing me, Lucas threw back the shot he'd taken from the tray. "If she is, she will magnetize to my heat and light. You'll know your answer, but it will come at a cost. I forged it. In my hands, it will be helpless to my will, just like it was yours."

Frowning, Aureus considered me and sipped his drink. "She must consent." Nodding his head in acceptance, Lucas downed another shot. Eyeing me, Aureus wet his lips, tempting me to taste them. "Have you ever been shared, Danse?"

Affected by the alcohol as I was, I burst out laughing. "I started my life as a god's concubine, remember? A hedonist god. Parties would go for months, and orgies were the norm. Maybe if I'd come to be in a later period, I'd have been more concerned with such behavior, but I arrived a blank canvas, and the image Dion painted on me was that pursuit of pleasure in all its forms can never be shameful —as long as all parties involved are adults and consenting. A 'do what ye will, as long as it harms none' approach to life."

Both of them had their brows raised now. Then, smirking, Lucas grabbed another fluorescent shot glass from the tray of a passing waiter and threw it back. "She's going to fit in just fine around here."

With his eyes still on me, Aureus licked his bottom lip. The temptation to crawl into his lap and kiss the living hell out of that mouth had me getting all hot and bothered between my legs. Remembering my lack of underwear and sitting on a satin skirt that would show any wet stains, I stood up. Grabbing a shot glass, I threw it back, the burn not even bothering me at this point.

"I want to dance," I proclaimed as I set the glass on the small table between the brothers.

"Then go dance." Aureus dismissed me, then he went back to studying the other revellers.

Giving me a wink, Lucas grabbed another drink and joined his brother in watching the festivities. Rolling my eyes, I wandered into the throng of writhing bodies, arms in the air, hips already swaying.

❖

The Best Drug

Rolling my head back, I lifted my arms and gave myself over to the music. The couple in front of me stopped their make-out session to check me out, both of them eye-fucking me hard as they dry humped on the dance floor.

Cold hands grabbed my hips, and then a hard torso was pressed against me, encouraging me to grind against him. Which I did, smiling and loving the familiarity of this setting. Dion would love this party.

Around me, people danced in a way that mimicked sex. Hell, the couple in front of me would have made Dirty Dancing fans blush. It turns out that ghosts get very touchy-feely when they can get hands-on living flesh and be touched in return. The music seamlessly merged from one song to another, not allowing the perception of time to burst the bubble of beats and gyrations on the dance floor.

After I'd been dancing so long that others near me had taken the bump and grind to penetrating levels, Lucas appeared before me. Until then, I hadn't even noticed the couple that had eye-fucked me were all but naked and fucking hard with the beat of the music.

Slipping his hand along my jaw, Lucas stared into my eyes, probably to catch the flare of heat racing through my veins that his touch caused. Breath rushing out of me, I went to him as he stole me away from the ghost whose hard-on had bruised my ass in our dancing. He was unimportant now. Only Lucas and his heat echoing inside me mattered.

"You've had me before," I panted as his fingers on me came surging from somewhere in my memory. The way he held me in his hands, hammered me to his satisfaction, then admired the thing he'd made.

"I forged you," Lucas corrected as he turned us, drawing me closer to him. "You were the most beautiful weapon I ever made for someone else. Born of my light magic and forged in the eternal flame, your purpose was singular: to dispatch evil souls straight to Hell. With you in his hands, Aureus no longer had to take the time to ferry the judged between realms and into Hell. Instead, you found and dispatched them for him."

Tilting my head, I stared into the blood-red of his pupils, something long and shining with golden light reflected back to me from the depths. "I was a weapon, not a living being?"

"You lived, even in your previous form. You pulsed with life the moment I quenched you, before I'd even finished shaping you. While creating you, I fell into a delirium. I was not aware of anything around me or what my own hands were doing until I held you finished in the palm of my hands. Aureus used to tell me you hummed to him, that when he grew lonely, you sang to him and guided him to the evil he sought, comforting him, and allowing him to return sooner."

Caressing my throat, Lucas stared into my eyes, his thumb tilting my face up, his body against mine, making me pant from the burning need inside of me. Turning me around, Lucas held me tight to the front of him.

"Dance. I want to feel you rub up on me like you did that spirit."

Being guided by Lucas's hands on me, I opened myself to the music and wound my hips in time with the beat. "That's it. You're still beautiful to look at, and the way you feel in my hands... I have no doubt you were the Spear of Lost Souls I forged many millennia ago."

Sweeping a hand up, Lucas cupped my breast and started massaging it. Arching into his hand, I dropped my head back on his shoulder. Taking the offer, Lucas nibbled and kissed my pulse.

His hand started scrunching up my skirt. "Do you glow when you come?"

Biting my lip, I moaned as his free hand found the skin of my hip, then slipped forward to cup the heat of my sex. "I bet you are blinding when you climax."

Pressing into his hand a little further, I turned my face to peer back at the gorgeous angel behind me. "You tell me."

Lucas dove forward with a smirk, catching my mouth in a kiss that could drive the sanity from the most sensible of people. Turning in his arms, I used his jacket to pull him closer to me. Moaning, Lucas slipped his finger through the wet gully of my sex, then drove it into me.

Breaking free of the kiss, Lucas grinned as he fingered me hard and fast. Shifting position slightly, he kissed and licked my neck while I clung to him, his heat melting my core.

"My brother loved you, and I was a little jealous that I hadn't kept you for myself. But I love my brother, and you gave him something no one else could, so I would never have taken you back. Even now, when you light my desire in a way no mortal could, I can't fathom taking you from him. Not when I saw how forlorn he was when he lost you last time."

Clinging to Lucas's shoulders, I struggled to find my words. "Why?"

"Hmm," Lucas grunted as he added a second finger to his endeavor. "When I needed Aureus, I used you to manipulate him to do what I wanted, and it cost him dearly. I got sent to oversee Hell, but they took you from my brother to punish him. I watched them throw you into the eternal flame, watched your light fade as you turned molten, heard you scream as the flame undid you. Aureus cried for you. We were sure you'd been destroyed."

"But I wasn't," I breathed as Lucas brought me closer to release.

"The flame reforged you. I think you absorbed Aureus's love for you, and when the weapon he used on my behalf had to be destroyed, the flame returned you in a form my brother could love physically."

"But you weren't there when the flame finished with me."

"No." Lucas thrust his hand faster, harder. "And our brother found you instead and hid you away."

Growling fiercely, Lucas yanked away from me, shocking me in the sudden loss. Taking my wrist, he weaved us between the writhing bodies of the orgy that had been carrying on around us. At the side of the room, Lucas yanked me forward and turned me. The momentum slammed my back into the wall, knocking the breath out of me.

Not waiting, Lucas scrunched my skirt up, then dropped to his knees. Eyes going wide, I lifted my face to the ornate ceiling and cried out as he sucked the hood of my clit, then tongued it while he finger-fucked me hard. Cursing, I lifted a thigh to his shoulder. My core tightened, and my legs started shaking. Knocking the goat skull from his head, I fisted his hair and came harder than I could ever remember.

While my eyes were still closed, a mouth smashed down on mine. A smile bloomed on my lips, recognizing Aureus straight away. Wrapping my arms around his neck, I took the kiss deeper, moaning as his hands caressed me while he moved me with him. When I opened my eyes, Aureus dropped back onto his sofa, threw his cloak open, then took my hips and helped get my skirt out of the way as he guided me to straddle him.

Capturing my mouth, Aureus kissed me heatedly, his fingers finding the two buttons that held my dress in place behind my neck. As soon as he released them, the dress fell off my shoulders, and it took little encouragement from Aureus to bare me from the waist up.

"She lights up when she comes," Lucas chuckled, caressing a hand up my bare spine.

Gods, the two of them touching me was more than I could handle. My blood caught on fire and burned through my veins, melting away all thoughts and hesitation.

"I saw. It's how I found you," Aureus responded dryly, his eyes and hands all for my breasts making me hum for him. "She's definitely my spear of lost souls."

"Was your spear," Lucas chuckled. Grabbing my hair, he forced my head to the side and kissed my pulse as his fingers slipped down my spine, over my ass, and found my dripping sex again, making me gasp. Swiping his fingers backward, Lucas pressed against my puckering. "Do you want us to sheath ourselves in you, Danse? Do you want to be ours again? For us to fuck you for all of eternity?"

Was there any possibility of saying no to the two of them? Even if my brain was online and capable of reasoning through this pleasure, my body was lit up like a fucking Christmas tree in their hands. There was no saying no to this level of euphoria.

"Yes."

Turning my head, Lucas kissed me again while Aureus dropped his mouth to suck at my peaks. My body jack-knifed in their hold, and Lucas used the moment to press his lubricated finger in, preparing me for what was going to come. And with both of them lavishing me with adoration, I was going to come again pretty damn quickly.

Slipping his hand down my abdomen, Aureus covered my sex and rubbed me. Moaning, I rocked against his hand, taking Lucas's finger deeper in my ass as I did. Dropping behind me, Lucas kissed down my spine, then pushed me forward and started tonguing my starfish.

"Fuck!" I panted. My cunt flooded and pulsed with need.

Watching how I rocked on his hand, Aureus growled low, then used his free hand to massage my breast.

"So, damn beautiful," Aureus muttered, then his hands were busy with his pants.

Kissing back up my spine, Lucas nibbled at my pulse again. "I bet she never glowed for her past lovers like she does us, that's for sure."

Grunting, Aureus grabbed my hips and tugged me forward. Feeding his cock into my slit to find my opening, he buried himself in me hard, forcing my breath from me with the size of him slamming into my core.

Wrapping his arms around me, Aureus crushed my mouth to his and kissed me with the same ferocity he was fucking me. It was frantic and harsh, and I couldn't get enough. My hands roamed and clung to his body while I rocked my hips with the same enthusiasm for building the mind-blowing sensation spreading through my body with every thrust.

A tug on my hair made me lean back.

Supporting my back with one hand, Lucas encouraged me into a backbend, then fed his cock between my lips. "Get me nice and wet, Danse. So I don't hurt you."

Letting go of Aureus, I grabbed the thick base of Lucas's dick and sucked the tip.

"That's it," Lucas encouraged, rubbing his hand down my sternum before massaging my breasts, squeezing a little harder now that they bounced with the ferocity of Aureus' fucking.

Even as a god's concubine, I'd never experienced anything like this. I'd been fucked eight ways from Sunday before it was even called that day. By multiple men simultaneously. But nothing in my very long history even came close to how exquisite it was to be the meat in the sandwich of these two beings. I'd started my life as a slave to the lust of a hedonist god, and millennia later, I was sucking the devil's cock while death fucked me into oblivion.

When my spit covered his shaft, Lucas pulled out and returned me to Aureus's arms.

"Slow down, Aurie. Let me join the fun," Lucas encouraged as he got his positioning right.

Grunting, Aureus stopped the hard pound. Holding me tight to him, he stared into my eyes. "Are you okay? Tell me if we get too rough."

Adoring that he would check in with me, even though he'd been pretty lost to his lust a moment ago, I caressed his jaw and smiled. "I've never been better."

I might have spoken too soon because neither of these guys was even close to average. So when Lucas pushed into me, I was definitely feeling just how big they both were. Cursing, I bit my lip and mewled a little as my body sucked him in as deep as he could go.

Pushing back some strands of my hair, Aureus watched me. When I clenched on the discomfort, he twitched inside of me, causing all sorts of pleasure to radiate out to my limbs.

"Good?" he asked.

"Very," I moaned as he did it again.

Smirking, Aureus gathered up my hair into one of his big hands and my breast in the other and used his hold to move my mouth to his.

"I've never fucked another celestial," he murmured against my lips. "I don't think humans will ever be enough again."

No kidding. "Good. I want the two of you for the rest of eternity."

A grin spread across Aureus's handsome face as Lucas

nipped at my pulse again. "Happy to agree with you both. Now, let's get back to the fucking."

Turning my head, Lucas kissed my mouth, tongue darting a taste. Slowly puling back, he started fucking me just as hard and fast as Aureus, making me cry out to a specific god of pleasure.

Moaning, Aureus pulled me close, sucking and biting at my neck. His hands added to the hard and fast pounding, both of them matching the beat of the loud music. Closing my eyes on the growing light around us as my body walked the tightrope of ecstasy, I held on for dear life, trying hard to wait them out. But when both of them groaned and lost their rhythm, I couldn't hold back any longer. Throwing back my head, I cried out my pleasure as it shattered me into a billion pieces.

A loud buzz filled my ears. A solar flare hurled through my body, detonating in my core, the heat filling me in cataclysmic pulses that rippled out to detonate my euphoria once again.

In the wake of the best orgasm of my life, everything was quiet and dark. Slowly, the heavy beats of the music filtered in over the heavy breathing of the two men still inside me. The moans and giggles of others were further in the background. So too were the clinking of glasses and conversations of those over near the food tables.

Kissing the nape of my neck, Lucas withdrew, then dropped onto the sofa right beside us. "Fuck! That was better than I expected. I might have to steal her from you, Aurie. Maybe I should take her into the depths of Hell with me and fuck her all day and night, neglecting my duties in favor of continuous pleasure."

Grunting into my neck, Aureus didn't object. He just held me to him, dropping sweet kisses to my neck as we both caught our breath. Combing his fingers into my hair, Lucas turned my face to his, and he kissed my mouth with slow intensity. With a final nip at my bottom lip, he slouched back and clicked his fingers at one of the waiters.

"I need a fucking drink to come down from that high." Taking a shot off the tray, he smirked when the waiter checked out his still semi-hard dick laying slick against his defined abdomen. "You like what you see?"

When the waiter swallowed, Lucas got a glint in his eye. "I'll let you suck it, but you need to be polite and lick my daughter's ass clean on my behalf."

"Daughter?" The waiter choked, his eyes widening, having obviously seen the display.

"I made her, so, daughter is the right term, isn't it?" Lucas feigned confusion for a second.

"I am not the fruit of your loins, so no," I laughed.

"How do you know that? Maybe I quenched you in my magical cum, and that's what breathed life into you in the first place." You had to give it to him; Lucas could keep a straight face while he spewed bullshit.

"Do we need labels?" I sighed, still happy, snuggled against Aureus while he peppered my neck in his afterglow.

"You're right, no labels." Turning his wicked grin back on the waiter, Lucas lifted a brow. "Come now. Our cum is seeping out of her with every second you stand there gawking. That's three lots of angel crack and all of us High Order. You can't get shit that good in your realm, so don't go wasting it. Hell, get a glass and save some for later."

"You are seriously disturbed," I groaned at Lucas. Then I gasped because the super-keen human did indeed get on his knees and start lapping up every bit of cum there was to have.

Chuckling, Lucas slapped my ass, making me jump, and then he gave it a hard squeeze, making me yelp a second time.

"I'm the prince of Hell, Danse. And I didn't lie. Celestial secretions are a drug to humans. It's how so many of us make them our slaves. He's had it before." Lucas indicated the guy who was pulling apart my cheeks and now tonguing around Aureus's base in his search for more. "I could tell by the look in his eyes. You can always pick the Angel cum freaks."

Grunting, Aureus shifted me to pull free, holding me above him and looking down my midline. "Don't touch my dick. He said to clean her."

Apologizing profusely, the waiter started licking and sucking me again, using his fingers in his eagerness to get as much as he could. The moans and slurping sounded quite animalistic.

"Once he's done, I'm taking you upstairs and washing you clean of his spit," Aureus whispered while glaring at Lucas.

Leaning forward, Lucas brushed his palm across my nipples, making things tighten below. The waiter moaned louder and grew more eager. Smirking, Lucas stared into my eyes.

"Danse, come on the poor boy's face." Then he pinched one of my nipples and chortled as I cried out in pleasure and came on the addict's tongue.

By the time Aureus helped me get my dress back in place and my legs beneath me, the waiter was so off his face, he couldn't stay upright to get the reward Lucas offered.

That's when I got the answer I had been searching for. As I gazed upon the high-as-a-kite waiter, I saw the look on my past lovers' faces. My ex loved eating me out after I came for him. Insisted on it every time we fucked.

"My last husband was a serial killer. I found out after he died. So I've been wondering why he loved me when he killed others. He was an addict to my climax, wasn't he? That's what saved me."

Giving me a wink, Lucas tipped his glass at me. "You're welcome. You didn't even need to ring the doorbell."

How he knew the question that brought me searching for the doorway to Hell, I didn't know, nor how he knew that I'd wondered if there was a doorbell. It didn't matter because the search not only gave me that answer, but also the one I'd been asking since my first resurrection. But, most importantly, seeking answers brought me back to them.

Putting a knee on the sofa, I kissed Lucas, soft and gentle, loving the quiet moan he released.

Glancing down, I noticed his cock starting to harden again. "Stay with us?"

Flicking his eyes to Aureus, Lucas blew out a long breath as he set his empty glass aside. "I have to go by sunrise."

"Everyone does," Aureus answered. When I stiffened, he swept his arm around my waist and kissed the top of my head. "The guests. You are not a guest."

"What am I?"

Staring down into my eyes, Aureus brushed his lips over mine. "That's up to you this time."

"Is it?"

Rising out of his seat, Lucas eyed the clock above the mantel. It was already three in the morning. Taking my hand, he kissed my temple.

"Like Aurie said. You have to consent. It's getting late. We can talk about logistics another time."

All Souls Day

~∾~

THE BED SHIFTING MADE ME STIR.

"You're not going to say goodbye?" Aureus asked.

"The sun is rising."

"Luc, we need to discuss this."

"I'll come topside again tomorrow."

"My curse—"

"You've still got another day."

Cracking an eye open, I waited for the grey light of the dawn to be bearable, then opened them fully. Across the room, Aureus stood buck naked, arms crossed, and face pissed-off while Lucas sat half-dressed on the love seat, lacing up his shoes. It was a beautiful sight to wake up to. I don't think anything could eclipse it. Okay—if Lucas was also naked and they were both about to climb back into bed with me, that would be perfection.

Cringing a little, I eased myself up, holding the sheet to my chest. My body felt delightfully abused from the night's activities. "Hey." Both of them looked my way. "What are you arguing about so early?"

Standing up, Lucas swept his suit jacket around and settled it into place. "I have to go." Coming forward, he put one knee on the bed, cuffed the back of my neck, and dropped a toe-curling kiss on me.

Grabbing one of his lapels, I moaned with longing for him. When he pulled back, I mushed my lips together, savoring the feel of him. "You'll come back again, right?"

Smirking, Lucas nose-booped me. "Tomorrow." Dropping his eyes, he frowned a moment. Then, reaching over to the bedside table, he opened the drawer and retrieved a pen before coming back to me. Grabbing the sheet, he yanked it down to expose my breasts, then started drawing something just below them, on the base of my sternum. "If Aureus has to go out and something happens. If someone comes here and tries to take you away, put your hands over this symbol and say my name. I'll get here as quickly as I can."

Lifting a brow, I combed my fingers through his hair while he drew. "And who would bother to come here and drag me off? No one even knows I'm here."

Sighing, Lucas lifted his eyes to me, the red beacon in the depths of his pupil getting brighter. Oh shit! He was actually worried it might happen. When I glanced at Aureus, I observed the same concern on his face. "This house sits between the here and there. It's a gateway between the realms, if you will. It's how humans can come here. But, it also means other celestials will sometimes pass through here. Most will not bother with you. They will likely think you are an earth-locked ghost like Isabelle at first glance, but if they look a little closer, they will realize you are not, and they will be as curious about you as we were."

"Can't I just tell them I am Aureus's girlfriend or something?"

"No!" Both shut that down quickly.

My mouth dropped open, and suddenly I wasn't so comfortable with the naked thing. Pulling the sheet up to cover me, I sat up properly. "What aren't you telling me?"

"We are fallen, Danse. You can't claim you belong to either of us. Avoid speaking or interacting with another celestial if you can."

Taking a moment, I looked between them. "Maybe I shouldn't stay here alone. If Aureus needs to leave, I should go back to the epoch realm. I can get a cabin up at Cradle Mountain for now, and then maybe find a place nearby where you can come to me."

Glancing over his shoulder at Aureus, Lucas exchanged a look with his brother, then gave me a soft smile and kiss. "I'll be back tomorrow. We can discuss it then." Going to his brother, Lucas squeezed his shoulder. "Walk me out."

With a glance my way, Aureus grabbed up his pants from last night, yanked them on, and then they left.

Not sure what to make of what was said, I went to the bathroom. After washing my face and hands, I examined my body for all the pleasure marks from last night. Finger tracks, fuck bruises, and teeth marks. Every single one of them bringing a smile to my face.

Circling my finger around the pentagram at the base of my sternum, I studied the symbols. The language was still in use when I was reborn, so I knew whose name it conjured, and it wasn't Lucas. "The Morning Star."

Not that it was a revelation. I knew last night who I was fucking. But, again, I'd been around in the years following the fall of the Angels. Even the gods who visited Dion's temple of pleasure talked about it. By the time Christianity emerged, the truth of the fracturing was lost except to the immortals who lived it. They rewrote history, making Lucifer the bad seed whose jealousy of humans drove him to become a power-hungry demon.

To think a celestial could ever be jealous of a human. It's like suggesting a wolf would leave its pack because it was jealous of a rabbit they ate earlier that night. The two are not connected. That much I knew.

Going to the window that overlooked the harbor, I watched the first light breach the horizon. As it did, Lucas left the house and walked the white gravel path towards the cliff. A longing I'd not felt before rose in my chest. Frowning, I absently fingered the symbol he drew on me. Slowing his steps, Lucas stopped and turned to look over his shoulder. Frowning, he eyed his shoes for a moment, then jogged down the stairs out of sight.

Lips kissed the nape of my neck as Aureus cuddled me to his chest. The tension of watching Lucas leave vanished immediately. Sighing, I leaned my head back onto his shoulder. "This is going to take some getting used to. No one has affected me the way you two do."

Kissing my temple, Aureus tightened his hold. "The feeling is mutual." Turning his face a little, Aureus breathed across my ear. "I want to make love to you. Will you let me?"

Blinking at the request, I pressed my lips together and considered the request adequately. It was easy to say yes to such a thing after centuries with humans as lovers, but I was a god's concubine. Dion was particular on the rarity of a god wishing to be intimate with someone for an emotional connection. Fucking was just that, and it rarely meant more to a god. I suspect that was the case for a celestial.

Turning in his arms, I gazed into Aureus's eyes. The lighthouse glow was very dim in the darkness of the night sea of his pupil. The thing is, intentional or not, there was emotion in the cracks of our interactions last night. Yes, the fucking was three horny beings pursuing our desires with each other. Still, that urge was founded on an existing connection. The way Aureus held me after he came, the way they touched me in the shower, and the way both of them wrapped me in their arms to sleep were fuelled by that emotional connection deepening.

Going on my tiptoes, our lips connected gently, pinching several times slowly before I tilted my head, and the tip of my tongue tasted his. Winding my arms around Aureus's neck, we kissed like that for several minutes. When we let it fall, our arms still holding each other, bodies pressing together, I met Aureus's eyes again. "I'd like that."

Taking my hand, Aureus led me back to the bed, urging me to lie next to him. For a long time, we kissed and touched each other, learning the contours of each other's bodies. We noted the areas that got a reaction and enjoyed just being there with each other. No talking, just touch, taste, smell, and sight to connect us.

Eventually, Aureus rolled me onto my back and lay between my legs. Gently, he pressed into me, taking his time, slowly rocking his hips as he kissed me intently. Caressing up his back, I enjoyed the slow burn of heat in my veins, the way every touch, kiss, and stroke made my senses come alive. Last night had been like jumping off a cliff into a bonfire. Today, making love to Aureus was lowering myself into a warm bath. We didn't rush it. Instead, whenever one of us came close to losing control, we'd pull back, slow it down, and change positions.

Facedown with Aureus laying over my back, I moaned long and loud. Pushing back a little, I sought permission to chase the needy itch, becoming desperate in my core. Groaning, Aureus stilled as his cock pulsed inside me, one of his hands grabbing my hip to stop me rocking against him. "Not yet," he panted against my ear. "This isn't how I want to come with you. Not this time."

Slowly, he withdrew, his breath rushing from him as he did. Kissing down my spine, Aureus caressed my ribs, waist, hips. Moving away, Aureus sat cross-legged on the bed. "Come here."

Crawling to him, I wrapped my legs around him, biting my lip as Aureus slid deep inside me. Using his hands to nestle me against him, Aureus wrapped me in his arms, and we sat there kissing slowly. Unable to stay still, I squirmed my hips in small circles to scratch the itch of yearning that was demanding more inside me.

Breaking the kiss, Aureus rested our foreheads together, holding me tight to him. "Do you remember anything about me from your previous form?"

Smiling quietly, I took his hand and moved it around me until his fingers brushed my spine. "This. Your fingers running over me. The way you held me securely, wielded me with skill, looked after me like I was precious."

"You are." Aureus sighed, fingers playing along my spine, making me hum for him. "You used to hum to me then too. I should have recognized that first. It hasn't changed."

Lifting my eyes, I stared into the depth of his darkness. "I've longed for you. I didn't know it was you until you kissed me the night you came for me, but I longed for something I knew I'd lost all this time. Dion knew. He used to watch me stare out at the sky, and he'd asked me what I longed for. It's why he told me that as much as he would hate to lose me, there was something I needed that he couldn't give me, and I needed to go find it."

Caressing my face, Aureus watched me. "Did you never give up?"

"Many times. I've gone back to Dion more times than I can count, but I always get restless and leave again." Smiling sadly, I traced the definition of Aureus's torso. "He's one of the lucky gods. Humans have never lost their lust for pleasure in all its forms. He's moved into modern times as much as your kind and grown stronger for it. He's never resented my wanderlust."

Threading his fingers into my hair, Aureus pressed my forehead to his. "No more. You won't need to wander, longing for me anymore. We've found each other again. I won't lose you a second time, especially now that I get to love you like this. Say you'll stay."

Meeting Aureus's intense gaze, I wet my bottom lip. "I will be wherever you ask me to be. Whether it be here, or if I have to follow you across the realms. I don't care if I have to wait for you in Hell. I will if it means I never have to be without you again."

Impassioned by my words, Aureus kissed me fiercely. Our bodies rocked together, the need for each other driving us now. There was no more waiting, no more holding back. Breathing heavily, the intensity of our feelings for each other was a twisted elastic band between us. As we gave in to it, it spun out of control.

Grabbing my hips, Aureus rocked our bodies hard and fast, his cock swelling and throbbing as he lost himself to his pleasure. Through it all, our eyes stayed locked with each other. The intensity of his gaze, the feeling of him coming deep inside, and the connection forged at my creation collided inside me, burying me in emotions I never thought to feel. Crying out as I came, I held on for dear life.

Truthfully, I was terrified the fervor that I felt with Aureus would make me dissolve into nothing. As I regained my bearings, I stared into Aureus's eyes. I sobbed once, a tear escaping in the overwhelming emotions we'd just released.

"Danse?" Aureus caressed my cheek, wiping away the tear.

"I'm scared I'll lose you again."

Shaking his head a little, Aureus clenched his jaw, then drew me tight against him, our bodies fitting perfectly together. "That's not going to happen again. I promise, Danse. I'm never letting you go."

A Secret Affair

"Aureus!" I sang to the headboard, then I tumbled into ecstasy. Grunting, Aureus thrust harder and faster. Yelling his praise, he tensed and cursed as tremors wracked his entire body.

Blowing out a harsh breath, Aureus collapsed on top of me, lips kissing along my sternum and collar bones as we recovered. We hadn't left the room all day, Aureus getting the chef to bring food up to us instead when we needed recovery time. Not that it lasted long. Keeping our hands off each other was proving impossible.

Turning his head, Aureus groaned. "I have to go."

"Go?" I asked, confused. My legs were still wrapped around him, so there was little chance of him going anywhere.

"I'm still a soul summoner, Danse. I get two days off a year. All Hallows and All Souls. My time is up."

"But you're just going to work for a few hours, and you'll be back, right? You're not going-going."

Shifting above me, we both gasped and cursed at the sensation with our bodies still joined together. Meeting my eyes, Aureus smirked. "I have two days of work to catch up on, but

I will be back. I just can't say how long it will take." Caressing my jaw, Aureus frowned. "What you suggested, about finding somewhere to stay close by in the epoch realm. I think that's a good idea. There is a village just on the other side of the harbor. You could get a room at the hotel for now. Then, when I get back, I can come and find you there, and we can sort out something more permanent."

Frowning, I eased my legs free of his waist. "You don't want me to wait here for you?"

Cupping my cheek, Aureus sighed. "If I could be sure you would be safe here, I'd insist you stay, but I can't guarantee your presence wouldn't cause issues. I might be gone for two or three days."

I accepted that answer—plus, I didn't want to be trapped in a strange house for that long without him. "Okay." Looking at the clock, I sighed. "But I doubt I'm going to get a room at this time of night."

Smirking, Aureus kissed me tenderly as he withdrew. "Sleep here tonight. In the morning, have breakfast and make your arrangements. Leave me a note telling me where to find you."

Staying the night here without Aureus sleeping beside me did not appeal. Getting out of bed, he headed to the bathroom. Rolling over, I grabbed my phone from the bedside table and connected to the internet. "Where are we? I might call now and ask about a room. Anything above a four-star hotel, and they'll have a night manager."

"Strahan," Aureus answered before he turned on the shower. By the time he was dressed and ready to leave, I had a reservation. "How did you go?"

"Good. I have a room, but check-in isn't until tomorrow afternoon. So I'll hang out here in the morning. Then, hopefully, Lucas will show up, and he can take me to the hotel after lunch and let you know which room you can find me in."

Smiling, Aureus leaned over me. "Sounds like a plan. Try and avoid the serial killers, okay?"

Grabbing him by his shirt, I pulled him down on top of me, loving the way he laughed as he fit his body between my thighs without thinking. "I'm going to miss you the moment you walk out the door, so best you leave a lasting impression."

Smile filling his face, Aureus caressed me through the sheet that kept me modest. "If I still had a Spear of Lost Souls, I could dispatch souls straight to Hell and get back to you faster."

Blinking at the suggestion, I pondered the dilemma. "Why did they take me away? Why was that the fitting punishment?"

All humor leaking away, Aureus pulled back and turned to sit on the side of the bed. "When the war broke out, Luc needed an army. I misused you, collecting evil souls before their time to swell the ranks of Hell. Luc then used those souls as his soldiers. Really, dispatching evil souls early saved their would-be victims, but the number one rule is that we can't interfere in mortal lives. So, they took you from me. Since Luc opened the gates of Hell, they banished him there, making him the warden of the judged, and Hell his home."

"And how are you cursed?" I asked quietly, wondering if it was all connected.

He didn't answer straight away. After a moment of sitting with his head hanging, Aureus swallowed hard. "They took my wings." He sighed painfully. "This house is the only place, other than Hell, that I can access in the celestial realm. Luc got Hell; I was sentenced to be the keeper of the grave gate until one of the betrayed forgives me. But none of them did. They've since been reincarnated and forgotten, so they couldn't forgive me for betraying my station even if I could convince them to. This is as good as it gets for me, Danse. If you chose to leave the epoch realm and wander the summer fields, neither Luc nor I could go with you. I am the grave keeper for the rest of eternity."

Touching his shoulder, I wanted to hug him, but Aureus stood suddenly. "I have to go. I'll see you soon." Then, unable to look at me, he left.

"You keep checking the time," Isabelle complained from where her ghostly form sat perched on the dining room chair opposite me.

"Shouldn't you have solid form in this realm?" I asked, ignoring her comment.

"I didn't cross. While you sit there all immortal in the celestial realm, I'm still in the epoch realm, so that makes me all ghost."

"Oh." Pushing my plate away, I sighed. "Lucas was meant to come and see me today, but I have to leave soon."

Pouting, Isabelle hung her head. "It sucks that you have to leave. I like having you here. Did you enjoy the party?"

"I did."

"You'd be one of the few to enjoy getting ass-fucked by the devil," Isabelle chortled. Then, after a second, she composed herself, sighed, and got serious. "I thought you were like me when we met."

"Except I wasn't see-through."

"Well, a lot of newly dead still look quite alive. You saw the ghosts at the prison. The priest was still pretty substantial, and he's a good two centuries deceased now."

Accepting that answer, I paused and glanced at Isabelle. "How old are you?"

Smirking, Isabelle tilted forward and cocked her brow. "Not as old as you." Well, she had a point there. "You were seriously a god's concubine?"

"Still am."

"Then what are you doing here?" A deep voice came from the kitchen door.

"Az!" Isabelle smiled, getting up to greet the Angel taking up the doorway. His appearance was almost an exact replica of Aureus, except his pupils hazed in blood-red as he looked me over. "This is Danse. She came for the Halloween party, but she's leaving today. Danse, this is Aurie's twin brother and the soul summoner for those without a guilty conscience, Azariel."

Spit filled my mouth as the Angel who found me on the temple steps eons ago stepped into the room. Smiling, I checked the time and stood up. "We know each other. Nice seeing you again. My ride should be here any minute."

Blocking my exit, Azariel pierced me with his gaze. I'm sure had I been human, he'd have weighed my soul, but since I didn't have one... "You didn't answer my question. What are you doing here?"

Clearing my face of emotion, I raised a brow at his attitude. "Wanderlust."

"That tells me nothing."

"It tells you all you are entitled to know."

His gaze was piercing, searching my eyes for answers. "How did you end up at the party?"

"Me!" Isabelle jumped forward, trying to distract him. "I invited her. I recognized a kindred spirit, so I invited her along."

Eyeing me, Azariel glanced at Isabelle, then used his finger to lift my chin and examine my neck. A zing of familiarity shot through me at his touch, memories of more than just my rebirth flashing in my mind. "You fucked my brother."

"Which one?" I snipped, turning my face to release his hold.

"The only one that counts when it comes to you."

Smirking, I gazed up at him through my lashes. Touching the lapels of his button-down, I stepped into his personal space, lowering my voice to a sultry purr. "I fucked several men at the party. That's what orgies are about, after all, so you'll need to be specific."

Frowning, Azariel considered me, then where my hand was caressing the lapels off his shirt. When my fingers slipped below the collar and cupped the heat of his neck, Azariel swallowed a little harder. "Aureus."

"Hmm, yeah, we fucked." Batting my lashes, I moved closer still, my body pressing against his. Then, dragging my hand down his chest, I pressed the back of my hand against the mark on my sternum. "He shared me with your other brother, Lucas."

"Lucas? You mean Luci-"

"He's going by Lucas this century," Isabelle cut in, floating just to the side, observing.

"And a human who used his tongue to clean us all up afterward. He really enjoyed your brother's sloppy seconds, if you get my meaning?"

"Addicts," he scowled.

Going up on my toes, I breathed along his strong jawline, feeling him harden against me. "Are you jealous?"

"Of an addict?"

"Of your brothers sharing me? Or do you now hate desiring the pleasure you found with me?" Smirking wickedly, I rubbed my hand over the hard lust in his pants as I lowered my voice to a whisper. "Don't worry, I didn't tell them."

Jaw clenched tight, Azariel cupped my face, his breath getting heavier as his desire grew. "About how I found you?"

"About how you bargained my life away while I was too confused and innocent to know better. How you indentured me to lust, with the only condition being you could access me whenever you desired."

Lips hovering above mine, Azariel groaned. "Good. They wouldn't understand."

"Oh, I think Lucas would understand better than you think."

Turning quickly, Azariel slammed me against the wall, his thigh pushing between my legs, rubbing against me.

"You are still so fucking beautiful," he growled, hands groping me eagerly. "You were dropped at my feet like an offering from the gods. It took everything in me not to fuck you by the fire of the temple that birthed you. The desire you imbued in me set fire to my loins. But you were innocent then. That would have been wrong."

"So, you took me to a place to become a woman whose only purpose was to seek pleasure."

The smile on his face was growing. "Was I wrong? Have you suffered there?"

He was right. The lifestyle never chafed at me, never bothered me. "No. It was probably the best place for me at the time." Then, tilting my head, I wondered. "Why did you stop coming?"

Blowing out a breath, Azariel backed up a little to meet my eyes. "The jealousy abated. And after a thousand years, so did my anger. That's when the guilt started to churn my stomach."

"Guilt for what?"

"For watching his brother pine for something he couldn't have, knowing full-well it was within his power to give him," Lucas answered from the foyer.

Backing up quickly, Azariel glanced at Lucas, then at me, and closed his eyes. "Fucking hell!"

"Language, Azariel. Only us fallen can be so crass."

"Don't start, Luc."

Casually moving toward us, Lucas eyed me. Adjusting my clothing, I smothered the quiet smile trying to make itself known. Turning his stare on his brother, Lucas cocked a brow. "You stole her away for yourself." When Azariel flashed a glare at his older brother, Lucas sighed. "I guess I wasn't the only one jealous of our baby brother and his spear."

Forehead creasing, Azariel snapped his head to Lucas. "You were jealous?"

"I often resented ever giving her to him. But then, his life was so much harder than ours, I couldn't bring myself to take his one item of happiness away either. But, apparently, you could."

"It was his punishment."

"And now? He'll never go home again, never be able to stay anywhere but this gateway permanently. His curse to be the grave keeper is eternal. Would you make his loneliness eternal also?"

Considering me, Azariel cleared his throat. "Maybe we should discuss this in private." When Lucas nodded once, Azariel stepped forward, caressed my cheek, and dropped a kiss to my forehead. "You said your car was waiting. Travel safe. I'm sorry I stopped coming to see you. I hope you didn't take it personally?"

Huffing, I chuckled a little. "Not at all. I thought you were dead."

"Hmm," Azariel hummed as if he didn't believe me, then strode out of the kitchen.

Coming forward, Lucas kissed my temple, then dropped his mouth to my ear. "Don't go too far. You've given me leverage, and I'm going to use it to bring you home."

As the brother's disappeared from sight, I blew out a breath and turned my eyes to where Isabelle sat eating popcorn. I mean, it was going straight through her to the ground, but it was pretty funny, just the same.

"OMG! The drama. What do you think will happen? Will

they duel to see who gets to keep you—and hello! What's with not telling us you used to bang Az?"

"Because the first thing I was going to tell Aureus is that his twin hid me away in a temple of pleasure and kept me as his secret mistress for millennia."

Chewing her lip, Isabelle's face softened. "Did you fall in love with Az?"

Inhaling, I couldn't bring myself to answer. Did it hurt when he stopped coming to see me? Yes. Would I consider what we'd had together love? Not when I compared it to what I'd experienced with Aureus yesterday.

"I should go." Grabbing my bag, I went out, hoping my car was still waiting for me.

Immortal Concubine

ANSWERING THE KNOCK AT MY HOTEL ROOM DOOR, I exhaled roughly when I saw the handsome man leaning with his shoulder into the frame, his head resting there too.

"You don't look happy to see me," Dion assessed.

For an extremely old god, he barely looked thirty. His blond hair was lighter than usual, his golden skin tanned, his hazel eyes bloodshot. He wore jeans and a polo shirt, and the fact he had shoes and a shirt told me he'd either left a party to come here or was heading to one. Either way, if Dion was here, shit had officially hit the fan.

"Azariel called you, I gather?"

"He did," Dion answered, using his arm on the frame to straighten up. "You going to let me in?"

Huffing, I threw open the door and went back into my suite.

Two days I'd waited here for Lucas or Aureus to come and tell me what was happening, but neither had shown up. So today, I'd gotten out to do some sightseeing. Strahan was a beautiful wilderness, and I didn't want to miss out on the opportunity to see it. After sailing the harbor and a trip up the river to the forest boardwalk, I understood the attraction of living here.

Going to the bar fridge, I grabbed two drinks and handed one to Dion as he joined me. Putting a hand to my lower back, he kissed my lips, and when I didn't linger, he stepped back and took a large swig.

"So, this is the greeting I get after a century?"

"No offense, but I'm kind of shitty you are here."

"That, I gathered. Want to tell me why?"

"Because I hazard a guess that you are here to revoke my travel visa and take me home."

"Give me a reason I shouldn't."

"I'm in love." Frowning, I stared at the drink in my hand for a second. "I want to be with him, but he's a fallen angel and a soul summoner." Licking my lips, I closed my eyes. "He's who I've been longing for all this time. I was his before the fall, and they took me from him to punish him."

Pursing his lips, Dion glanced down at his half-empty bottle, then at me. "This would be Azariel's younger twin, I take it?" When I nodded, Dion jumped his eyebrows. "Well, that explains the call from Azariel."

Cringing, I set the bottle aside. "I'm sorry he made you leave whatever party you were hosting. You could have sent one of your lackeys to call me home."

Setting his empty bottle aside, Dion leaned his bum back on the bench and crossed his arms. "Danse, in all the times you have wandered, have I ever demanded you return to me?"

"No."

"No. So, why would I send a sycophant to do it for me now? I think that showing up personally, leaving Ibiza in full swing, would be a better indication to you of how fucking serious this situation is. Wouldn't you?"

Closing my eyes, I bowed my head. "I'm sorry."

When Dion remained quiet, I lifted my watering eyes to meet his.

"Are we leaving immediately?"

Tilting his head, Dion stared into my eyes. "I don't think I've ever seen you come close to crying."

Looking away, I closed my eyes for a moment to try and get control of my emotions.

"We're staying the night. Azariel wants to meet with me tomorrow." Wandering over to the bed, Dion looked it over, then back at me. "Should I get my own room?"

Shaking my head, I swiped at a tear. "Actually, I don't want to be alone."

Cocking that damn brow again, Dion pulled his shirt over his head and dropped it to the floor. Inhaling deeply as my eyes traversed him, I couldn't help but reach out and trace the definition in his musculature.

Over the years, Dion's physique had become the desired appeal of the general epoch population. Grabbing his jeans, I stepped into him and used my thumb to pop the top button open.

"It hurt leaving him. It's never been like that before."

Combing my hair back with his fingers, Dion moved me closer. "That's telling in itself, Danse."

"I don't know if I can come back."

Lowering his mouth to mine, Dion kissed me agonizingly slow. "Don't think of that right now. Instead, show me how you feel."

Yanking open the fly of his jeans, I went to my knees. Taking Dion's beautiful cock in hand, I took everything I felt and used it to express myself to him.

Later, Dion spooned me from behind, slow deep strokes driving me to find my ultimate pleasure. Slipping his hand to my pearl, Dion brought my mind back to where it needed to be.

"Let go, Danse. Give over to those emotions twisting you up inside, and let go."

Rocking against his palm, I reached behind me and grabbed Dion's hip.

"Harder."

Giving it to me a little more, it still wasn't enough.

"Harder."

Fisting my hair, Dion yanked my head back.

"Trust me, Sweetness. Now give me my sugar." Pinching my clit hard, Dion released it and shifted his hand to my hip as I tensed and came for him.

Afterward, Dion held me in his arms, snuggling me against his chest.

"What happened, Danse? Tell me everything."

While we were at the cafe down the road the following day, Dion's phone rang. Glancing my way, he picked it up. "Yes?" He listened quietly for a moment. "I have, yes. She's with me now. I will discuss it with her, and I will give you my answer when I am ready." Again, Dion fell quiet. "This is not the same era, Azariel. Women are no longer the property of men. As it turns out, she was never yours to bargain with, so I will discuss what will happen with Danse, and then I will come to the table with what I feel is a fair trade. We'll be ready by lunchtime."

Hanging up, Dion put his phone down, then sat back. Looking around us, he sighed long and hard. As the last of his breath left his lungs, so did the noise of others around us. They continued unfazed, but they couldn't hear us now. "Over the years, how many concubines have I taken in, Danse?"

Frowning at the strange question. "Um, probably fifty, in my time. You may have had others in my absence."

"I haven't." Licking the foam of his cappuccino from his lips, Dion met my eyes. "How many have I kept around long term, for the extent of their lives?"

Swallowing, I looked away from the intensity in his eyes. "One."

Nodding, Dion set his cup back in its saucer. "Pleasure can never be forced. It must be consensual for both parties. If I had sensed any reluctance when Azariel brought you to me, I would have rejected you. You were scared and innocent, but you were a blank canvas I could work with. And by giving you a home, I knew I would be protecting you from any further harm."

Frowning, I stayed quiet, listening to Dion's explanation. "I say further harm because it was apparent you had been traumatized. I questioned Azariel about it, and he admitted that you were a celestial that was punished as one of the fallen. That you were thrown into the eternal flame of the afterlife and emerged as I then found you. No name, no memory, no history. But I knew for you to be punished, you had history.

"I pushed Azariel, but he promised me you were neither a willing participant nor at fault for what occurred during the revolution. He told me his brother betrayed your trust in him after the rebel angel manipulated him. I am not one to trust a single point of truth, so I checked his story. Only once his brother's part in the rebellion was confirmed by multiple sources did I agree to his terms."

Taking a sip of coffee, Dion licked his top lip again. "I let him think the favor was for him, but I did it for you, Danse. Every concubine I took in was to protect a woman from external forces in her life. I taught them true pleasure, and all of them eventually found love and asked me to let them go. I did so happily. Their ongoing pleasure was a thing of power for me. Only you never found love and asked for your freedom. Maybe it was because you were the only immortal concubine I had. The first time you left to wander, I expected you to never come back, or to find love and ask me to release you. But you came back. As time after time, you went in search of your longing only to return to me, I came to accept that maybe you were where you should be."

When Dion stopped to take a sip of his coffee, I nodded. "I felt the same," I admitted.

Dion nodded as if he knew that. "I've grown attached to you, Danse. It isn't love, but a friendship after all these millennia together. You have always come back, and I think I made the number one mistake in a relationship and grew complacent. I accepted a thousand years ago you would wander, but in the end, you would always be mine."

"Is this your way of telling me you won't let me wander anymore?"

"No. No. I would never restrict your freedom like that." Taking a breath, Dion met my eyes. "Azariel wants to renegotiate the terms. He wants me to free you into the care of him and his brothers. They want you to come live with them, splitting your time between the three of them in the Celestial realm. If it's what you want, I'll grant it, but I wish to put forward my own case."

Still reeling from the revelation I could be with Aureus if I agreed to be shared between them, Dion's request, instead of a demand, threw me for a loop. "Your case?"

Wetting his lips, Dion chuckled. "Yes, Danse. In today's society, you are my wife. I wish you to remain so. After all this time, you are my best friend, and your company is a type of pleasure not easily found with humans. It is more than lust, and I don't wish to lose it completely. I am not asking for you to come back to me full-time. I don't think my lifestyle suits you for too long anymore, but I would still like you to make time for me, even as a friend."

Blinking, I chewed my lip, staring into the coffee wrapped in my palms. "And I have to decide this now?"

"We are due at the grave gate for lunch. They will expect to begin negotiations with me after the meal, if not during it. What they don't realize is that this was always going to be your decision."

"Okay." Getting up, I met Dion's eyes. "I'm going to go for a walk. What time do I need to be back here?"

"I'll meet you back in the room at twelve." Getting up, Dion eyed the harbor. "I might try a tour."

Setting off in opposite directions, I sorted through everything Dion told me. Then I started a pros and cons list because there was no other way to try and make sense of this without one.

An Eternal Choice

‹••›

THE GRAVE GATE WAS A BEAUTIFUL WHITE HOUSE perched on the cliff overlooking Hell's Gate. It didn't look as big or grand as it was inside—but then, it was a gateway into the epoch world. You entered through the front door, and the two realms overlapped. Step off the back porch onto any of the two white gravel paths, and you were wholly in the celestial sphere.

Inside is what mattered. The large hand holding mine gave a gentle squeeze, shifting my attention from the house to the handsome god beside me. "Are you sure of your choice?"

Swallowing hard, I gazed at the house again. "Yes." Focusing back on my longtime companion, I squeezed his hand back. "I know you are biased, but would you tell me if you think I am making a mistake?"

Inhaling, Dion pulled me closer, caressed my cheek, and tilted my face up to his. He was taller and definitely more imposing than the celestials. Not that it was so apparent that he walked into a room and everyone wondered who let the hulk out of his cage, but his presence surrounded you in that way.

Truthfully, I think he was going all out for the meeting with the celestials. Dion usually downplayed it with the mortals. They thought of him as a wealthy playboy billionaire kid who was happy to share his fun and toys with others. If they knew their fun made him more powerful, they'd probably think twice.

Staring into my eyes, Dion pressed his forehead to mine. "I wouldn't have accepted your decision if I thought it so flawed, Danse. You are my concubine; your wellbeing is still a concern for me."

"Did you ever check up on me when I wandered?"

Smirking, Dion dropped a kiss on my lips. "Always. You had shit taste in mortals, Sweetness. You gave your sugar to the worst kind."

"Apparently, I was forged to seek out evil and dispatch it swiftly. Aureus believes my taste in men was that base coding in play. I was attracted to the evil before they fully gave in to it. Apparently, they became addicted to me because celestial cum is a drug for mortals. Then they unraveled quicker than they would have without me in their lives."

"Not just mortals, Sweetness. Celestials fuck like bunnies because they can't get enough of each other either. And there is a reason I called you 'sweetness'."

Surprised by this, I stared up into his eyes. "Really? Even you?"

"I can't get addicted, but you are better than anything the mortal realm has ever produced. The gods love celestial crack as much as everyone else."

"Oh, my, god! That is what Azariel meant when he offered you unlimited pleasure with me. It wasn't the sex—"

"Yes, it was. Because without the sex, I don't get my sugar."

"He was dealing me as a drug."

"Yes, Sweetness. Unlimited access to the ultimate ride and high. I definitely got the better end of that deal, if I do say.

Once I got you broken in, you rode my dick all day and night for a month. I'd never come close to being exhausted, but you definitely gave it a hell of a try. You still do when you come home."

Smirking, Dion pinched my cheek where heat rushed. Sex was all I knew and had, so that's what I focused on excelling in. I could distract myself better once the written word, music, and other knowledge came around. However, sex with Dion was still my favorite pastime.

Cuddling me against his chest, Dion watched me. "Sweetness, you're delaying now."

"I know."

"They are waiting and are just as keen to get you alone with them."

"They are going to be disappointed."

"Your choice is what is best for you; that's all that should matter. If they care about you, as they claim. If you are more than the addiction of celestial crack soaking through the thin skin of their balls and entering their bloodstream, they will understand."

"Transdermal absorption."

"Yes, that." Tilting my chin a little more, Dion kissed me slow and deep. When he drew back, he gave me a wicked grin. "No more delaying. The faster we make this deal, the faster I can be feasting on that sweet nectar of yours. If I get my way, I'll get to lick your pussy while one of those pricks is buried deep in you on the lunch table."

"Dion!" The heat racing through my veins at the suggestion would not keep me level-headed. "Now, my panties are all drenched."

"Good." He tugged my hand and walked me up the path to the front door. "Let's get this done."

Aureus opened the front door and, with no concern for Dion, wrapped me up in his arms and held me tight. Clinging to him, I sobbed against his chest. "I'm sorry. I only got back yesterday, and Luc and Az told me what had happened. We needed to sort things out between us before moving forward."

"He means they've been beating the shit out of each other after finding out one hid you from the others," Dion chuckled in the ear not pressed to Aureus's chest. "I'm Dion. Danse's husband. You must be the prick that abused her and got her taken from him."

"Dion!" I laughed, unable to stop myself. He was like this. He was blatantly honest when it riled people up and honey-lipped when he was setting a trap.

"It's okay. He's right." Aureus eased back on the hug but didn't remove his arm from around my waist. "I'm Aureus."

Smirking, Dion stepped inside and took in the foyer. Azariel and Lucas stood further inside, arms crossed, looking not too happy. "You two should thank your baby brother. My Concubine's feelings for him are the only reason I even agreed to this meeting. Otherwise, we would have been back in Ibiza by now." Dion settled his eyes on Azariel. "And I would have told you to go fuck yourself. Your access to her expired long ago."

Jaw tensing, Azariel glanced at me, then Aureus, then bowed his head once to Dion. "Lunch is ready." Turning around, Azariel marched towards the dining room.

"Huh, I didn't think anyone could annoy Az as much as I do. I'm Luc."

Barely nodding his head, Dion observed Lucas. "The rebel angel, prince of hell, master manipulator, and the true person at fault for what befell Danse."

"Yes, yes, guilty as charged." Lucas grinned, sidling closer. "But you forgot god-killer. And if I hadn't done all of that, she'd still be a spear, and you'd have never gotten to spend how many millennia plowing her for your pleasure."

"The pleasure was mutual. It must always be mutual in my

temple," Dion corrected, taking a step closer. "You forged her?"

"Yes."

Gazing over me, Dion smirked. "You do good work." Putting his hand out to me, Dion grinned wickedly. "Sweetness." Leaving Aureus's arms was hard, but I was still Dion's. Once my hand slid into his, Dion turned his shit-eating grin on Lucas. "And I thank you for inadvertently setting the ball in play that would bring Danse to me. I value her immensely. She is very precious and irreplaceable to me."

The smile dissolved from Lucas's face. Instead, his eyes flicked to Aureus with concern as Dion led me towards the dining room without a backward glance. "Don't look back," Dion murmured. "Make them think the worst, so they are more willing to accept our proposal."

Pressing my lips together, I gripped Dion's hand and prayed it worked out.

"I want her back," Azariel answered bluntly after Dion suggested we not waste time once the meal was finished. While we'd eaten, the tension had been so thick that I could barely breathe.

"Just you?"

Glaring at Dion, Azariel gritted his teeth as he inhaled for patience. "No. The three of us want her to be ours. We'll share her between us, with Danse spending time at each of our homes."

Lifting a brow, Dion looked at Lucas and Aureus. "You will let him remove her from you a second time, take her beyond where either of you can go, and trust him to return her when he should?" When those two glared at Azariel, Dion set his sights on Aureus. "And you will let them take her to Hell to live. To trust the master manipulator with the woman you claim to love in that place of torment?"

"I would never hurt her," Lucas snarled.

"You all have a job to do, Prince Warden, which means Danse would be left alone for long periods down there. I believe the Raquie still abode in hell as the guards also? Would you trust other fallen to mind their manners with her? To seek her consent?"

The red haze of rage in Lucas's eyes was enough of an answer. Clearing his throat, Aureus called our attention to him. "You make good arguments for why Azariel's plan is flawed. I admit I shared the same concerns."

"Then you'll understand that it is not a condition on which I am willing to negotiate. Two angels at this table have already proven they cannot be trusted. Their jealousy of your affection for Danse when she was a spear already hurt her."

Aureus sat back, his eyes moving between Dion and me, and where he held my hand on the table. "You're not going to release her, are you?"

Meeting Aureus's eyes, Dion lifted a brow. "No. The deal I made with Azariel was for eternity, and I will keep the precious gem he sold to me for that long." Azariel cursed; Lucas and Aureus glared at their brother. "However, Azariel did negotiate access to Danse whenever he wanted it. I am willing to extend the agreement to include the two of you. I've checked with Danse, and she is happy to take the two of you as lovers." Dion indicated Lucas and Aureus.

"The two of them?" Azariel snarled, his eyes locking on mine. "Not me?"

"Not straight away," I answered. "You hid me from your brothers for millennia. You don't get me back so easily. You made them wait, and so you will wait."

Gritting his jaw, Azariel glared at me with those intense

dark blue eyes that all three brothers shared, his pupils flashing red. "For how long?"

"How long did Danse scream in the fire while the eternal flame remade her?" Dion asked. When Azariel snapped that glare to Dion, Dion chuckled. "It was months after the war ended before you brought her to me. How long was her torture?"

"I knelt in the temple listening to her scream for five days before they dragged me here to the grave gate," Aureus mourned. Then, lowering his head, pure misery evident in the slouch of his body and the drop in his shoulders.

"Seven days," Azariel answered. "She screamed non-stop for six days and six nights, and on the seventh day, I found her on the steps as she is now."

"Ah," Dion sat back, smiling at the ceiling. "The seven-day creation rule is still observed. Although, in this case, it might have taken that long to unmake a celestial weapon forged to be eternal."

Taking a moment, Dion slowly lowered his face from whatever thoughts consumed him, picked up his wine, and took a sip before nodding his head.

"Seven years. It's really not that long to wait for an eternal being. Still, I'm sure it will be torture knowing your brothers are constantly visiting her on my island and taking their pleasure from her."

"We are not gods. We cannot travel on thought. We must fly across the earth. Granted, we use gateways between the realms like this one to travel a lot quicker. Still, the closest gateway to Ibiza is in France," Lucas argued. "Aureus's wings are cursed to only exist in the epoch realm and only for him to retrieve a soul. He can't travel the celestial realm to hasten his travels or fly to her. It is not good enough. Danse needs to come here to the celestial realm. She needs to live with us."

"She will not be living with you," Dion clarified. "Especially not in Hell."

"This is unacceptable!" Azariel growled.

Picking up his wine with his free hand, Dion cocked his brow. "You haven't even come near her in nearly two thousand years. At least these two had an excuse. What was yours? You hurt her when you just stopped coming."

Silence fell around the table.

"As previously stated, I am not giving her up. A concubine is the equivalent of a wife. I care for Danse deeply, and I will not let her go. Nor will I negotiate a situation that puts her at risk of being hurt—" Dion's eyes landed on Lucas, "—or stolen again." His eyes settled on Azariel with a glare, letting him know there was no trust.

"The agreement on the table is for Danse to accept you as lovers. You will be able to visit with her, but it will be in a location within my reach and in which her safety can be guaranteed. In Ibiza, you can stay with her for as long as you desire, I don't mind, but sharing is a must if you do. If that does not suit you, suggest somewhere else that meets the requirements."

"Here," Aureus answered. "Here at the grave gate. It is within easy reach for all four of us. Only Azariel posed a danger to her here because only he knew her origin story. Danse can stay here when she is to spend time with us."

Squeezing my hand slightly, Dion resisted smirking, having manipulated the angels exactly to the suggestion I'd made. But there was one element still to explore. "I feel that suggestion is acceptable, to a point," Dion considered, swirling his wine. "There will need to be a time limit; otherwise, the three of you could claim it is always your turn, and I may never get her home."

Peering across the table, Lucas leaned forward. "It is a good suggestion on Aureus's part. What time frame would you impose?"

Dion took a sip of his wine and considered the three of them, then me. Then, lifting his hand that held mine, he kissed the knuckle of my index finger. "A month at a time, for a maximum of three months a year, and I'll include the three-day celebration of the soul door as a bonus for you. Of course, you may still come to my temple and see her any other time."

"That is inequitable for reasons we have already discussed," Lucas huffed back, his eyes glancing at Aureus—because that's who would lose in this deal.

"Maybe. Maybe not. Danse, you had something you wanted to say to Aureus?"

Taking the cue, I rose from my seat and went to Aureus. Frowning, he stood to meet me and took my hands in his when I offered them. "Danse?" Aureus watched me, his brow furrowing. "What is it?"

Wetting my lips, I took a breath, tears already escaping. "When Lucas manipulated you during the war, your actions had consequences for many. You used me to steal souls before their time, which led to my destruction. Yes, I was reborn, but I remember the pain when they threw me into the fire, the way I screamed for you as I was pulled apart. When I was reborn, that sense of utter betrayal and the pain stayed with me for the longest time. You did that to me. You betrayed my trust and love for you, and I've had to carry that with me just as long as you have."

Looking crushed, Aureus closed his eyes. "Danse, I know I deserve it for what I did, but I can't lose you again."

"We have borne the punishment of your actions for longer than man even remembers the truth of what happened. Finding you has been amazing and heartbreaking at the same time because you are cursed for what you did, and that curse will prevent us from being together."

When Aureus went to say something, I cupped his face in my hands, pressed my forehead to his, and whispered, "I forgive you." Our tears merged together as I hovered my lips beneath his. "Do you hear me, Aureus? You betrayed me, but I forgive you. I forgive you, and I love you."

A loud cymbal reverberated through the room. Crying out and covering our ears as the echo vibrated through us, causing me to fall to the ground, dizzy and disorientated.

Negotiations

As silence descended, I tried to get my bearings.

"Danse." A hand appeared before me. Taking it, Aureus helped me back up. When I was stable enough to look at him, Aureus stood tall, his massive white gold wings stretching behind him. Lucas and Azariel stood open-mouthed, gawking at their younger brother.

"Well, look at that. You were right, Sweetness. All that boy needed was a little forgiveness," Dion chortled. "Well, I believe that sorts the inequity issue. Do you agree to my terms?"

Staring down at me like I was the one who sprouted wings, Aureus had his mouth hanging open. "You knew?"

"I hoped. When you told me about your curse, it occurred to me that I remembered the pain that I suffered from your actions, that you had betrayed me—well, the former me. So, it made sense that I might be the one you needed forgiveness from. Even if it hadn't reversed the curse, I knew you needed to hear it."

Mouth still gaping, Aureus just stared at me. Then,

regaining his senses, he cursed and pulled me tight against him, kissing me until I couldn't remember my name.

"Aureus, we need your agreement." Azariel broke the moment. "Three months of the year, Danse will come here, plus the soul-door days. All other visitations occur wherever Danse is based, whether in her home with Dion or wherever they roam."

Still holding me, staring into my eyes, Aureus smiled. "If Danse is happy with that, I am happy to agree."

"Danse?" Dion prompted.

Clutching at the back of Aureus's neck, I bit my lip. "You'll come to see me regularly, right? Like, whenever you're not collecting souls, you'll be with me?"

Smile growing, Aureus hovered above my lips, the golden light strong and bright in the dark sea of his eyes. "Every moment I can be, I will be with you. I love you."

"I love you too."

Picking me up, Aureus set my bum on the dining room table, kissing me with such intensity I thought I'd burst into flames. Yanking at his pants, I shoved them from his hips while Aureus dismantled my dress.

Aureus rubbed his fingers over the drenched fabric of my panties. A growl echoed through his chest as he slipped his finger underneath the fabric, using his knuckle to part my folds and tease my nub.

Moaning into him, I rocked my hips and pressed harder to his chest while taking his weighty cock in my palm. He was too thick and long, and as I stroked him, I swiveled my wrist, massaging the bead of his longing into the silky smooth tip.

Breaking from my mouth, Aureus licked and sucked at my neck, his free hand cupping my breast and teasing the stiff peak of my nipple. Hanging my head back and side, I gripped his cock harder, turning my wrist at his base and then slipping down to caress his balls.

"Fuck, I love how you sing for me," Aureus groaned as his mouth travelled to meet his hand.

I didn't even realize I was humming, but it made me smile because it was a natural response to Aureus touching me. It felt so fitting, so ordinary after all this time without him.

My blood burned with need in my veins. As I arched my back for Aureus to wrap those lips around the pink flesh of my breasts, I caught the faint golden haze out of the corner of my eyes, bringing my attention to my subtle glow.

With a yank of Aureus's hand, he tore my panties off my body, making me jump with its violence, only to moan and curse loud as his cock rubbed through my wet lips and pushed inside my hot, needy cunt.

"So fucking beautiful," Aureus growled as he pushed into me. Stretching me around his girth until he buried deep with one last shove, forcing my breath from me with a curse and my nails to grip his golden skin.

Once he was inside me, Aureus brought his mouth back to mine. Then, with one final passionate kiss, he started moving —claiming me, making love, and fucking me simultaneously. Crushing my mouth to his, Aureus kissed me with the same ferocity he fucked me with.

Clinging to him, my legs wrapped tight around Aureus's waist, I couldn't remember ever being this happy. Every thrust built the tension in my body. Pulses of electrical pleasure sparked to every part of my body every time his pelvis grazed my clit, tightening my core.

Over Aureus's shoulders, his giant wings glowed brighter and brighter as he drove us closer to the edge of the cliff of ecstasy. Our bodies were pure light blinding us to everything around us but each other, the sun's fire growing hotter in my core.

Meeting Aureus's eyes, I stared into the midnight sea of his pupils. The golden glow of the lighthouse of his being shined over the jagged shore of his millennia of loneliness, guiding me home.

Aureus brushed a kiss over my lips, staring back at me, and in a voice so slow and deep that it vibrated my soul, he murmured, "Bring me home."

A solar wind blew through my core, tightening everything to the point of pain, making me cry out. Then, with one last pump of his hips, Aureus toppled us deep into the ocean of euphoria, our combined light blinding me as we found heaven.

Coming back to my body, Aureus held me tight in his arms, our chests panting against each other. Fingers combed into my hair before giving a slight tug, making me bare my neck.

"I hope you saved some of that light for me," Lucas murmured as his lips pinched my jugular, forcing my body to clench around Aureus's still hard cock.

Moaning, Aureus kissed me gently, staying inside me while Lucas caressed my body, reactivating the dying heat in my veins.

"You have to share, little brother." Lucas chuckled. "You'll get her to yourself enough after today, but you can't expect me to watch you two burn brighter than the sun and just sit there with my pulsing cock in my hand."

"I mean, I could." Aureus laughed against my lips. He gave me a wink, kissed me once more, and slowly withdrew. "But I'm not Azariel."

A grumble from the other end of the table made the two touching me chuckle. Aureus stepped back from me to give Lucas space between my legs but kept my mouth against him.

"Complain until the cows come home, brother. You brought this on yourself." Lucas snickered at Azariel before going to his knees and swiping his broad tongue right through my slit.

"Fuck!" I moaned, hanging my head for a moment, lightning pulsing through my core, immediately twisting it.

"Good?" Aureus asked.

"Very good."

Giving me a final kiss, Aureus went back to his seat, picked up his wine, and took a large mouthful as he collapsed butt naked into his chair as if he was a king taking his throne.

I didn't get long to admire the view because Lucas chose that moment to feast on the celestial crack that Aureus and I had created together. His tongue delved inside me, fucking me and licking my good spot in his desperate need for the high our cum provided.

"This is unacceptable," Azariel complained again. "Had I not hidden her, who knows what the council of angels would have done with her. She was taken from Aureus for punishment. Just because she was remade into a vessel of womanly delight would not have changed the punishment. They probably would have locked her away in hell to punish Danse for her part in a war she couldn't remember and had no say in her part of it."

Swiping his tongue through my folds, Lucas sucked on my clit until I cried out and gripped his hair, my eyes rolling back in my head. Then, kissing my inner thigh, Lucas rose to stand, cuffing my neck and bringing my mouth to his but waited until my eyes met his gaze.

"Az is right. While hiding you from us for this long was wrong, had he not taken you away, the council would have done much worse to you, no matter how innocent you were."

Gripping Lucas's shirt, I started working the buttons free. "You want me to wave his seven-year wait?"

Staring into each other, we breathed together. Then, finally, I pushed Lucas's shirt free of his shoulders, letting it fall to the pile of clothes that Aureus and I had already created.

Slowly, Lucas shook his head, the sides of his eyes crinkling slightly. "Not entirely. Just a stay of execution. What do you think, little brother?"

Unable to turn my gaze from Lucas with the way he had control of my head using my hair, I could only listen to Aureus's opinion. His would matter more to me than any other as he suffered the most with me. He'd loved me.

Aureus huffed, his voice somewhat muffled as if he spoke into his wine. "This is a celebration of finding Danse again, after all."

Raising his brow, Lucas waited.

"Dion?" I asked because we'd talked all this through before coming here, and changing the terms felt like something I needed his opinion on.

"I was not hurt by his abandonment, Sweetness," Dion answered, clarifying this would be my call.

Caressing down Lucas's muscular but lean body, I unbuckled the belt holding his pants in place. At the same time, I considered what a reprieve could look like that did not relent on Azariel's punishment.

As Lucas's pants fell to the floor and he brought his big veiny cock closer to kiss my sex, I licked my lips and nodded my head as much as Lucas's hold allowed.

"He can take pleasure from my mouth, but he can't put his mouth or cock between my legs for seven years. Take it or leave it."

"Az?" Lucas focused solely on me, using his hand to rub the dome of him back and forth over my nub and opening.

"You deny me the high of our joined pleasure?" Azariel checked.

"I do. I will take it from you, but all you will get is the physical pleasure of my mouth."

There was a grumble and a sigh. "I can kiss you, touch you?"

"Yes."

"Can I make you come with my fingers?"

Watching me, Lucas put his mouth to mine to cover his whispered, "No. He'll suck your cum from his fingers."

He'd cheat the system. But if I said no, I'd be giving without receiving.

"Yes," I answered, making Lucas frown. "But I'll suck your fingers clean. You can't ingest my cum for seven years."

A blood moon shone from the midnight sky of Lucas's pupils, the sides of his eyes crinkling. Then he buried himself hard and fast inside me and started fucking me like he had a minute to finish, or he'd lose me.

"Fine!" Azariel pouted at the other end of the table, making the others chuckle.

Keeping his grip on my hair, my eyes on him, Lucas fucked me hard, making me brace against the table behind me to stop from sliding back. My legs shook where they wrapped at his waist, the force of his fucking driving me quickly to orgasm, and as I cried out and came again, a grin split Lucas's face, and he closed his eyes to bathe in my glow.

"So warm. Like a tropical beach at midday," Lucas moaned, slowing his pace to a leisurely stroll while his hand moved from where it pinned my hip to cup my breast.

Dropping his mouth, Lucas sucked, licked, and teased the peak, sending bolts of pleasure to my core, prolonging my climax.

Three Angels and a God

OPENING MY EYES AS MY GLOW FADED, AUREUS stood behind Lucas and leaned over his shoulder, whispering something to him before straightening and giving me a wink.

Lucas lifted me off the table, turned, and swapped our positions. "Straddle me. This party is about to get better," Lucas muttered against my lips as he slid back to sit on the table. Then he kissed me while his hands caressed me, drawing more moans from my throat.

Fingers felt where Lucas and I were joined, touching me gently as Aureus's heat covered my back. Kissing the top of my spine, Aureus marked every vertebra with his mouth as he descended. Then, with his hand pressed against my back, Aureus forced me to lean into Lucas where he lay on the table.

With me exposed, Aureus spread my cheeks and touched his tongue to my puckering. I moaned as he swirled and pressed his tongue into me, taking his time to prepare me for sharing. At the same time, Lucas held and kissed me, pulsing his dick, eliciting moans where it rubbed deep against my cervix.

"Did you know there are nerve endings in your ass that,

when activated, can bring you just as much pleasure as my mouth on your clit?" Lucas asked.

Dion blew a raspberry as he laughed. "I'm pretty sure Danse has known that longer than most. She found her sexual awakening with me in my temple. Trust that I have chased that high in every way possible. Nothing you do will be new to Danse, but I'm sure she could teach you a thing or two."

When Lucas met my gaze, I smiled and lifted a brow before giving him a wink. Aureus chose that moment to delve the fingers he'd used to collect the cum seeping from me into my rear, tenderly pushing past the ring of fire and then scissoring to stretch me for him.

Biting my lip, I arched my back, and Lucas took the opportunity to bring my breast to his mouth and lathe it in worship.

"Danse, are you ready for me?" Aureus asked as he dropped kisses to the top of my spine.

"Yes," I moaned. Pleasure zinged through my body from the trifecta of stimulation the two provided.

Kissing over my shoulder, Aureus stole my lips, then pressed into me slowly. Coaxing my body to adjust to his size, competing for the space Lucas was already occupying through the thin wall that separated them. Lucas cursed when I clenched tight as Aureus found his depth, dropping his head back to the table, his hands grabbing my hips and urging me to start rocking over him.

"You feel so fucking good."

Aureus pulled me upright to press my back to his chest. His hands cupped my breasts, squeezing and teasing them as I rode them. His kiss dominated my attention and slowed my trajectory to nirvana.

"Sing for me, Danse," he begged as my hips rocked faster, my body tightening quickly, chasing the ecstasy I knew I would find waiting.

"Az, why don't you get your dick sucked already. I'll take celestial sugar for dessert," Dion encouraged. "It's not like sharing like this is new for you."

A moment later, a shadow closed over us, fingers touching my chin, gently bringing my focus forward and up to where Azariel stood on the table. He'd lost his shirt but only unzipped his pants, freeing the heavy burden of his desire.

With Lucas controlling my movements with his hands on my hips, and Aureus keeping me upright by holding my breasts, I reached up and took hold of Azariel's thickness. He wasn't as big as his brothers. However, he was still swinging a big dick. After meeting Lucas and Aureus, it matched what I considered to be the archangel alpha attitude.

Bringing it to my lips, I darted my tongue to taste his lust already leaking from the tip. Groaning, Azariel gripped my hair and closed his fist, but not in a way that hurt.

"I've fucking missed this mouth," he confessed, then forced my eyes to his. "It was the guilt that kept me away. I never stopped wanting you."

Keeping my eyes locked with his, I opened my mouth and slid him along my tongue, holding his gaze until he hit the back of my throat, cursed, and lifted his face to the ceiling. Then I closed my eyes and started fucking him with the same eager rhythm as my body took his brothers.

"Fucking hell!" Azariel moaned loud, his cock already swelling, making me eager to have him spill down my throat.

My blood heated to melting point, my body chasing the ultimate pleasure. Responding to my need, Lucas and Aureus started thrusting harder and faster, driving me quickly towards nirvana as my hand and mouth worked Azariel faster.

My mouth was full of saliva, my sex making the wet slapping sounds as our bodies collided. As my glow shone brighter, my throat vibrated with the song Aureus's hands played on me.

A white light fought against my golden glow where Azariel stood before me. Lucas was glowing with a pale blood-orange light getting brighter with every thrust from below. His eyes closed tight, his mouth panting and moaning louder as his cock grew and delved deeper.

Lightning branched through my body to my core as Aureus pinched and rolled my nipples, making me tighten around them as he leaned into me.

"You're so beautiful. A siren calling us to our end, the way you sing for me, Danse. It's my everything, and I've waited an eternity to hear it. I'll never lose you again."

Aureus shifted his hand to my prayer bead and made my song rise an octave. Then it was too much, and I cried out around Azariel's throbbing cock as I shattered into oblivion.

Pulling my face to him, Azariel yelled his pleasure as he poured down my throat. Lucas roared beneath me a moment later, his release drawing my orgasm to the next level. Aureus wrapped his arms around me and cursed as his body jerked hard behind me. Our combined light blinded me as I fell deep into the nothingness of euphoria.

"Wonderful!" Dion chuckled as I slowly came back to earth.

For a moment, I was lost, floating, and then Aureus kissed me slowly. The touch of Aureus's lips on mine anchored me back into my body, giving me substance. It felt just like the times I reincarnated after each death.

Fuck, I think I just died from orgasm.

"That's exactly how I was hoping this lunch would end," Dion cheered.

Breaking into a laugh, Aureus looked over his shoulder at Dion, still holding me, but easing the tightness of his arms.

"That! Was earth-shattering," Lucas panted beneath me, stealing my attention, his pupils still dilated as he rode the high. "Fuck, if I'd had you before the fall, I would never have concerned myself with Yahweh and his bullshit. Let him play the almighty; I would have kept you in my bed and never gotten out."

Pushing out of his chair, Dion grinned at me and gestured to the table in front of him. "Come on, Sweetness. Give me that sugar."

Smiling, I fell to the side, Dion catching me and easing me to lie on the table with a gentle chuckle.

"I've never seen you so high. I can't wait to join you." Then dropping to his knees, Dion took his tithe.

Later that evening, I was curled up in Aureus's arms in his bed. Downstairs, Lucas and Dion had started an impromptu party. The sounds of music and drunken revelry carried through the house, but Aureus and I were happy, wrapped in each other and the blankets.

Resting on his chest, I stroked my finger back and forth over his collarbone. "How long until I see you again?" Dion would take me with him in the morning.

"A few days. Are you okay with going home? You could stay here, make it our first month together for this year."

"Dion wants me to go home. I've been gone a century. He needs to introduce me to his current sycophants as his wife, and it always takes me a good week to settle into being back in the temple." Not that it was an actual temple anymore. Just a modern mansion with all the amenities a party house needs.

"Did you want me to wait a week and let you get settled?"

Smiling, I ran my hand up to his neck and lifted my face to meet his eyes. The midnight ocean stared back at me. Aureus was still a little high. Then again, with how much fucking we'd done today, so was I.

"No. I've gone without you long enough. So don't you dare stay away if you can be with me."

Caressing my jaw, Aureus brought our lips together.

"Your husband is a god!" A feminine voice moaned beside us suddenly. "Why are you bothering with angels when you are married to the god of pleasure?"

Breaking apart, Aureus and I turned our wide eyes to where Isabelle lay in bed beside us, still incorporeal but naked as a jaybird.

"You can fuck as a ghost?"

Isabelle rolled towards us, all happy and excited. "Not normally, but being a ghost is no obstacle for the god of food, wine, and pleasure. You have to bring him to visit with you. That way, I get more than one day a year to fuck and scream my way to orgasm."

Chuckling at the blissed-out look on Isabelle's face, I ran my fingers over Aureus's hard pecs. "I can't promise anything. He has a pretty full schedule and doesn't like to leave his temple unless there is a big ass party worth his while.

Grinning at me, Isabelle cocked a brow. "He's fucking Dionysus; the party goes where he goes. You should see the way those angels are partying downstairs. He's going to want to do this again. I promise." Then she fell back and floated above the bed beside us as if we'd all just fucked.

"Isabelle," Aureus groaned.

"Yeah?"

"This isn't your room, and it's Danse's last night here for a while."

Turning her head, Isabelle frowned at us, then watched as Aureus guided my hand beneath the sheets to his growing need. Her eyes widened. "Oh! Right. Sorry. See you next time, Danse." Then she dropped through the bed and disappeared just as Aureus solidified in my grasp.

"Are you sure she's not just lying beneath the bed?"

Aureus grinned. "No." But there was a twinkle in his eye.

Narrowing my gaze, I teased my thumb around his silken head. "Isabelle, are you under the bed?"

"Nooo," she answered, making Aureus and I start laughing.

Pulling my laughing mouth to his, Aureus paused, his eyes flicking to the side. "Fuck off, Is."

"Yeah, Is, Dion is looking for you," Lucas added beside the bed.

"Fucking hell," Aureus groaned as he pulled my forehead to his, closing his eyes in annoyance.

Isabelle whooped, and her presence vanished when the blankets lifted. Lucas pressed his body to the back of mine. My body rubbed them both with the way I was laughing.

"What, you thought you'd get her all to yourself on her last night?" Lucas chuckled as his hands took hold of my hips and lifted me to straddle him, making me yelp at the sudden repositioning. A moan quickly followed as Lucas slid all the way inside me.

"Sharing is caring," Lucas lectured Aureus.

Lucas kissed me as he rolled before Aureus could respond with a snarky comeback, putting us on our sides, inviting Aureus to take the big spoon wordlessly.

Lucas pulled back as Aureus cuddled into my back, his cock knocking at the back door, and looked over my shoulder. "Don't worry, Dion is keeping Az busy. It's just us tonight."

Caressing his nose along my shoulder and neck, Aureus breathed me in. "You okay with this, Danse?"

Reaching behind me, I gripped Aureus's hair and brought his mouth around to meet mine. "I love you. As long as I have you, I'm okay."

A grin spread across Aureus's face, his eyes glancing at Lucas for a second before they closed, and his lips captured mine in a toe-curling kiss. Then he pressed into me, and time became irrelevant in our joined bliss.

I'd found what I'd been yearning for since I'd been reforged. My home was with Dion. It's where I was safe, so I couldn't leave it permanently. I knew that I would be complete as long as I never lost my angels, the three brothers of souls; the blessed, the lost, and the damned.

Join the Beautiful and Deadly

Join Ebony's Mischief List

Sign up to Ebony's mailing list for the following perks:

- latest news on new releases
- heads up on upcoming promotions
- exclusive freebies like coupons to read Ebony's stories on Radish for free
- first chance at Giveaways
- get a free book

Go to https://ebonyolson.com for more information

Of Shadow and Light

Messina Doe was just looking for a warm place to spend the night. What she discovers is a place the human race had long ago buried and forgotten.

The dark Fey haven't forgotten humans. The throne room of the Unseelie court is the hottest underground nightclub around, but if you step through the wrong door, there is no going back.

No one ever escapes. Never.

Once, someone did.

Sink

❖

"Stop chewing on that," Lisa snapped yanking my finger out of my mouth.

"I can't help it. I'm freezing and starving," I murmured trying to keep the shiver out of my voice. Stepping to the side, I looked at the line to get into the club. It was too long tonight; there was no way we were getting inside.

Lisa went back to fidgeting with her blond curls. "Would you relax. Tirades will open soon. Half of those inside will leave, and we'll get in. Just chill. You will never survive the streets if you whine all the time."

"Chilling isn't a problem." Since the music was audible outside, I started dancing on the spot to keep warm.

Lisa had been on the streets for six months now. When we met a few weeks ago, she made it sound so much more appealing than my home situation, so I'd packed the measly belongings I owned and joined her. We spent the nights clubbing so we were inside and warm, and the days at the university, sleeping in the library or stealing people's scraps in the cafeteria between classes - Easier done than you would think.

You just carried a dishcloth, wiped a table as you collected a tray, and walked off.

Lisa's big brown eyes latched onto my hand as I lifted it to my mouth again. With a huff, she started playing with my dark hair. "We'll be fine, Mess. Stop fretting, okay?" Nodding, I forced myself to relax.

"Ladies." A man materialized out of the darkness next to us. Truthfully, he'd probably been leaning on the lamp post there, and I just hadn't paid attention to him until he spoke to us. Lisa's eyes widened, her shoulders rolled back so that her small breasts were the focal point in their push up bra. Knowing that move already, I lifted my eyes to see just how good looking this man was.

If I were to describe him, it would be in one word. Shadowed. The man was good looking, but to me, he seemed to surrounded by shadows which made him blurry and stopped me from really describing his features in detail. Dark hair, but no specific color, dark eyes that I wouldn't say were brown, and an average complexion. The man wore all black, so in the pale streetlight, the only color on him was his mouth. Red, as if he'd just finished eating pomegranates.

"You look like girls out for a night of fun. I'm heading to an underground nightclub that stays open till dawn. I wouldn't mind a beautiful entourage."

"What's the entry cost?" Lisa flirted while she sussed it out.

"Free," he advised, typing something into his phone. "There's food too. In fact, it's the owners birthday tonight, so he's catering."

He had Lisa's interest now. "Where's this club?"

"Just outside of town. I'm heading there now if you want to join me?"

Lifting her pale brow in challenge, Lisa scoffed. "Cause I'm stupid enough to go off with a strange man."

The man smirked. "There's a bus. It picks up other

patrons, so no one drinks and drives. The owner is very big on the safety of his patrons." He pointed up the street where a bus was approaching. It was painted black with purple neon lights along the sides. "I'm Gus, by the way." Stepping to the curb, Gus waved down the bus.

"Come on." Lisa took my hand.

"Are you sure?" Didn't she just mention not being stupid and going off with a strange man? The bus pulled up where a girl and three guys who were already waiting stepped inside. Laughter and music blasting out into the cold night from inside, offering warmth and safety. Gus put his foot on the first step and raised an eyebrow at us.

"I'm sure." Squeezing my hand, Lisa strode towards the bus.

Gus's smile was closed lipped, his eyes reflecting the neon purple side lights as he led the way on board. Lisa followed dragging me after her. As I reached the top of the steps, the heavily tinted doors slammed behind us. For a moment, my pulse thrummed in the side of my neck, making it feel like someone was tapping my carotid artery.

The scene before me was a busload of relatively young people having a great time on a party bus. My lungs exhaled with relief as skimpily clad girls danced, some trying to use the poles, guys cheered and laughed as they drank their beer, the atmosphere relaxed and not unlike any bar on campus.

Releasing a squeal of joy, Lisa shrugged out of her jacket as she headed for the seat Gus was saving for us. Taking a deep breath, my head spun under the onslaught of men's cologne and women's perfume filling the bus. Blinking rapidly, I shook my head till it cleared, dark shadows racing across my vision as I followed Lisa. My hand still captive with hers until we took our seats.

"Do you want a drink?" Signaling the man behind the bar, Gus noted Lisa's hesitation. "My shout."

"I'll have a beer. Thanks."

Nodding, Gus looked at me. "I'm fine for now, thanks. Drinking and moving isn't a good combination for me."

"Motion sickness?" When I nodded, Gus patted my leg in reassurance as he stood to go to the bar. His touch left a chill on the bare skin of my thigh causing me to rub it to warm it up.

Watching me, Lisa put her mouth to my ear. "Are you still cold?"

The bus was fairly warm by the layers all the other occupants were removed, but I always took forever to warm up. Poor circulation or some such. "What are you doing?"

"One drink won't hurt."

"We're underage. I don't want to get thrown out for drinking alcohol as a minor. We're just here for warmth and food, remember?"

"Shh! Like anyone could tell that looking at us." At only nineteen, Lisa was hot and could easily pass for twenty-one. When she graduated high school last year, her step-father kicked her out because she refused to earn her keep by letting him charge his associates to screw her. Lisa's attitude was if men were paying to have sex with her, she'd be the one making money, not her scum-sucking step-father. I admired her for that.

Everyone was partying and having a great time as the bus moved to the next stop and picked up more people. Busy watching Lisa flirt with Gus, it took me a while to notice we hadn't stopped in some time. Peering out the heavily tinted windows, I cupped my hands around my face to block the inside light from my vision. Trees.

"Something wrong?" A woman asked sitting down next to me. Jumping back from the window at her sudden appearance, I looked her over. She was beautiful, but like Gus, she had that shadowed sensation which stopped me making out any exact details. In fact, the harder I looked, the less detail I could see. Her eyes appraised me hungrily, lingering on my jugular.

Licking my lips, I created a little more distance between us. "We're not in the city anymore." The woman raised an eyebrow, eyes jumping to mine, narrow in focus. "Gus said the club was just outside the city, but I can't see anything but trees."

The woman smiled, her shoulders easing back a little. "It is. There are a lot of people arriving for the banquet, so they've asked the bus to drive around an extra thirty minutes, so they can stagger the entry and avoid a large queue."

"Oh." As inexperienced in clubbing or these sort of underground clubs as I was, I decided to accept the excuse. However, the nagging sensation everything wasn't as it seems kept grating at my nerves.

The woman exchanged a judgemental look with Gus. "This one has eyes of light."

"I realized that after she was on the bus."

Standing up, the woman shook her head as she moved away. "Watch her hands when the fun starts."

Tilting her head "What language are you speaking? It sounds cool when you speak it."

"How many bears have you had?"

Shrugging me off, Lisa ignored my whispered question and returned to batting her eyelids at the handsome enabler beside her.

"Eirnish." Looking past Lisa, Gus noticed my frown at his answer. Smiling at me, he reached out to tug at my jacket collar. "Are you cold?"

Unhappy to have lost Gus's attention, Lisa turned her shoulder to try and block me out. "Mess takes a while to warm up."

Tall enough to lean forward a little more and maintain eye contact, Gus waited out my answer. "Poor circulation."

Tilting his head in interest, Gus appraised me again. "Huh, me too."

The bus hit a bump the same time a loud mechanical noise started outside. Gus smiled as the bus came to a halt. "We're here!"

We let the others go first, then Gus put an arm around Lisa and me, and walked us off the bus last. We alighted into an underground car park filled with expensive sports cars. My eyes went wide. Whoever came to this club had money.

Turning my head towards the mechanical noise, I watched as the carpark gate closed and locked. Instantly, I started searching for an emergency exit, but other than the door we were walking towards, I couldn't see another way out.

Holding my tongue, I shivered in fear with a very uneasy feeling crawling up my spine like a venomous spider. The same feeling I had when my adoptive mother married Chris when I was six. She met him, married him, then died, all in twelve months. The turnaround left me with a stepfather who felt burdened with me, and a year later, a stepmother who detested me.

"Still cold?"

Shaking my head at Gus, I kept my mouth shut. The truth was, I was too anxious to feel the cold now. We stopped in line at the door where a big man was stamping everyone's wrist and scanning everyone's license. He physically placed everyone's license on a scanner and copied them. They were keeping an electronic database of everyone who attended the club.

Waiting patiently, Gus grinned at us. "When he asks, you want a red stamp." Giving him a lascivious smile Lisa batted her eyelashes.

Listening as the bouncer asked the drunk guys in front of

us if they wanted red or blue, I frowned at the lack of explanation. "What's the difference?"

Gus, yet again, studied me. "You know, no one has ever asked that question." Still failing to answer it, Gus stepped us forward letting Lisa hand over her license.

"Red," Lisa purred when asked. The bouncer winked at Gus and stamped a big red bat on Lisa's delicate wrist.

"Red or Blue?" The bouncer asked taking my license to scan.

"What if I don't like either color?"

The bouncer raised a brow at me. He, like Gus, tilted his head to study me. "She's different."

Side-eyeing me, Gus nodded. "I've noticed."

"Hmmm." The bouncer considered me. He took my wrist in his hand and turned up the delicate side to look at it. Brushing his thumb over my birthmark, his brow furrowed as he peered at my pale flesh and the purple mark that looked like intertwined hearts. "Looks like purple is your color." With another glance at my face, the bouncer opened a drawer and took out a different ink pad and stamp.

"A present for the birthday boy then." With a smirk, he stamped a black cursive **W** on my wrist while Gus chuckled.

"I'm sorry, what?" Glaring at them, I snatched my wrist back.

Both Gus and the bouncer stared at me. "You understood that?" Gus asked.

"Of course I did. I'm not stupid!"

"Mess?" Lisa looked confused. "When did you learn another language?"

Frowning at all of them, my eyes went back to Lisa. "You only had the one beer, right?"

Gus laughed, but it was a nervous laugh as he rounded us both up and headed inside. Exchanging a nervous look with the bouncer, Gus sobered as the bouncer picked up his phone while we walked inside. The heavy door slammed shut behind us, the noise reverberating through my body as if I was hollow and the sound of doom echoed inside me. It took everything in me not to turn around and run back out into the carpark looking for an exit.

Passing down a small dark passageway, we entered a large cavernous space. The roof was three stories high and consisted of gothic style arches that seemed carved into a natural rock ceiling. There were open areas for balconies on the upper levels, arching around the walls like the viewing booths at the old style theatres. All of them with their black curtains closed tonight.

Ignoring the music playing, I stood in awe of the room itself. It wasn't massive, possibly the size of my school gymnasium for floor space. One half of the room contained the dance floor and DJ. The other half held the bar, the long table of food, and some lounges and armchairs, on which, people were already getting tongue tied to each other.

Stopping at the edge of the dance floor, Gus smiled at us both. "Shall we dance?"

"You two go ahead. I'll get some food." Indicating the table, I stepped out of Gus's arm. Lisa mouthed thank you as Gus led her into the grinding throng of bodies. Slowly meandering my way to the food table, I took the path closest to the wall to avoid the crowds. Reaching out, I touched the stone look walls only to find they were stone. No one would bother duplicating the grit of touching earth for decoration, nor would you want to.

Above touch was the sense of earth. Taking a breath to stabilize as a pulse of balance flowed into my fingertips. With that one touch, I knew we were underground. Interestingly, the stone work soothed me a little. This was a place that had stood for a long time, that was used regularly, and that they intended to keep using. It's not the sort of work you do just to burn the place down to hide the mass genocide that took place inside like maybe a shed.

A sheer curtain hung behind the buffet table creating a semi-covered hallway between the table and the wall. A slight breeze stirred the curtains as a door opened behind them, a short woman emerging into the veiled corridor carrying a large platter of fruit. It was much too big for the small woman, and she nearly stumbled with it.

Catching the tray with one arm and her with the other, I helped her stand before I placed the fruit on the table. The woman looked at me with large black eyes, much too big for her face.

"Are you okay?"

She looked old enough to be my mother but only came up to my chest. Gazing around the room hesitantly, she then back to me. "Only the fruit is safe," she hissed, then dashed back through the door.

Frowning, I tucked my dark hair back behind my ear. "Okay...." Talk about weird encounters.

Looking over the table, I browsed the selections of cupcakes, various cheesecakes, fresh fruit, and cream at one end. At the other was steaming hot food that looked direct from a Yum Cha restaurant. Various dumplings, pork buns, and other steamed foods. It smelled and looked delicious. Watching others walk up to grab food, I eagerly waited for them to make a selection. Starving, my stomach vocalized how much it needed sustenance. Licking my lips, I was already making my selection in my mind, watching the others step to the side with their plates full. Finally my turn, I placed a pork bun on my plate.

"Yum, this is so good," murmured the guy who had gone before me. Looking his way, I froze. He was smiling and happy, but as he ate, the food in his hand changed to look rotten. Maggots squirmed over the meat inside, blood dripped down his wrist, and the smell was rotten eggs. Peering at the man's face, I realized I was wrong, he was a boy. He looked to be a year younger than my eighteen, and by the looks of his unwashed jeans and shirt, also homeless. Blood dribbled down his chin as meat juices would, and I watched a maggot squirm free of his lips on the blood.

Vomiting in my mouth, I dropped my plate on the table and ran to the bathroom just past the buffet table. Just making it into a stall, I puked bile. I hadn't eaten in twenty-four hours, so there was no food to vomit, but my body was going to try.

"Are you okay?"

Peering over my shoulder, I saw a stunning woman, shadows swirling around her. "Yeah, just reacted to a bad smell." I was going nuts, surely.

With a smug smile growing on her face, the woman walked forward grabbing my wrist. "Red or blue?"

"Black!" Snatching my wrist back, the woman frowned, her shadows howled around her, and for a moment, the beauty faded to expose gaunt, red-eyed paleness, like she was covered in talc with purple markings like tribal tattoos up her arms.

'Glamor is free.'

When I blinked, she was beautiful again. Examining the mark on my wrist, the woman snarled and stormed away from me. Flopping over the toilet bowl momentarily, I waited for the energy to hoist myself up. The needed to get out of here got me to my feet. Washing my face at the basin, I stared back at my turquoise eyes. My stepmother used to call them unholy demonic eyes, but then again, she considered me a slut's offspring or a fatherless bitch.

Stripping off my jacket, I looked myself over. Unable to ever get a tan, my skin was too pale. With how easily you could see my veins, I was basically translucent. My breasts were a bit more than a handful, then again, I had small hands, so maybe they were the average person's handful. My legs were long and gangly. The short dress I was wearing made them look even longer. The dress was Lisa's, I only owned two pairs of jeans, a couple of shirts, and a jumper.

My step-mother didn't believe in spending money on me for anything but the necesseties. Hell, she'd only bought me a bra because the school I'd been at complained that it was improper for a girl of fourteen not to own one. So I got one and had to wash it by hand every night. The underwear I was currently wearing was a five finger discount, the heels were left behind after a university party. At least my childhood prepared me for living in the university boiler room.

There were rich men here tonight. Lisa planned to try and get herself a sugar daddy, that was always her plan to get her life back on track. Maybe I should consider it. Assessing my reflection, I shook my head. "Not a chance. You're a mess, and no one wants you."

Nothing about me was going to score me a sugar daddy, not when there were natural beauties like Lisa out there. Scowling at myself for even considering it, I grabbed my jacket and went back out to the nightclub. Still hungry, I remembered the lady saying only the fruit was safe, so I decided to give it a try. If it sprouted maggots and blood, I was out of here.

Grabbing a clean plate from the Buffett, I went for the fruit that everyone was avoiding. After piling my plate high, I retreated behind the sheer curtain and held up the wall while I ate. Nothing gross happened with the fruit, though, I deliberately avoided watching other people eat, focusing entirely on the food I was holding. When my plate was empty and my stomach satisfied, I focused on the dance floor.

Lisa and Gus were dancing like they were in the bedroom. Their hands and mouths all over each other. If it weren't for the clothes, it would be porn. Sighing, I hoped she found her sugar daddy. She'd been through worse than me and had more strength then I could ever possess. She deserved happiness.

"Happy Birthday, Ty!"

My focus shifted back to the buffet table to a group nearby. My breath caught in my throat. The man called Ty that everyone was congratulating was gorgeous. Truly gorgeous. No shadows were swirling around him to stop me seeing the detail. This man with his pale skin, tall, slender build and his sharp bone structure, was appealing in a way no other man had been for me before.

Appearing to be late-twenties, he was dressed all in black. Black shiny slacks, black shiny collard shirt, a black jacquard jacket and matching tie. He walked with a black walking cane, though, he didn't use it for support, and he walked like he owned the place.

"Nice party you've thrown," the man he'd just murmured something too praised. The owner. That's what Gus had said. It was the owner's birthday. This man, Ty, was the owner.

My wrist itched. Looking down, a small purple glow was emitting from the black ink stamped on my wrist. Confused, I looked up to watch Ty prowl the buffet, but not even considering the food. He was focused on the faces of the females filling their plates and stomachs. By the looks of them, they were homeless too.

My wrist burned as Ty came parallel with me, only the curtain and buffet separating us. Ty glanced at me. His deep-set dark eyes made darker by the shadow of his brow. The overhead light threw a shadow on his high cheekbones, making him look positively gorgeous and dangerous all at once.

He observed me between one step and the next. My wrist pulsed with the purple light from the ink burning into my flesh. Grimacing from the pain, I closed my eyes and bit my lip to stop from crying out. Suddenly, the pain was gone. Looking up, so was the owner.

'*A present for the birthday boy then.*'

Fear pounded in my heart. The cursive W was no longer a stamp on my wrist, but a black and purple tattoo, etched permanently into my flesh.

Read Of Shadow and Light

Dark Fantasy / Paranormal Romance by Ebony Olson

Romance Suspense by Ebony Olson

Hotel Series

HOLLY CLAIRE TRILOGY

Holly's Trilogy: Books 1-3 Hotel Series

(Compilation of Henderson, Cassidy, & Holmes)

JESS BUTLER TRILOGY

Best Sunset: Books 4-6 Hotel Series

(Compilation of Best Man, Best Layover, & Best Knight)

Standalone Books

Black Mark: The Complete Saga

Calypso

Rain: A Dark Past Romance

Protective Instinct

About the Author

Ebony lives in Sydney, Australia, with her husband, daughter, and six rescue cats. She loves to read fantasy, thrillers, and paranormal romance, spending most of her free time with her nose in a book or writing.

Having always possessed an over-active imagination Ebony spent her younger years regaling friends with fantastic stories, holding her audience captive with the passion and suspense of her characters plights. In adulthood, she shows no signs of stopping her imagination from spreading across as many pages as it can find.

Website: http://ebonyolson.com/
Ebony's Mischief & Mayhem Peeps

facebook.com/EbonyOlson.Author

twitter.com/Ebony_Olson

instagram.com/ebony_olson

amazon.com/author/ebonyolson

bookbub.com/authors/Ebony_Olson

goodreads.com/Ebony_Olson

www.ingramcontent.com/pod-product-compliance
Lightning Source LLC
Chambersburg PA
CBHW070332120726
47909CB00008B/2682